MW01484584

...SO SHE

Walked

Away

AVIYAH A. FORREST

Lightning Fast Book Publishing, LLC
P.O. Box 441328
Fort Washington, MD 20744
www.lfbookpublishing.com

Stay Connected with Aviyah A. Forrest at www.aviyahaforrest.com.

ISBN-10: 0-9974925-6-2
ISBN-13: 978-0-9974925-6-9

DEDICATION

To my friends and family (although the lines blur and there isn't too much distinction between the two), who've helped me look at my life, laughed with me at the absurdity of situations when they occurred, and loved me unconditionally.

CONTENTS

PREFACE

I wrote this book as a challenge to myself. I was recovering from a situation that had some similarities to the main character in the book and found myself with a lot of spare time on my hands. During that time, I began to study the Laws of Attraction and began to focus on changing the way I thought, both about myself and about life in general. The transformation that has taken place in my life in a relatively short period of time is absolutely amazing to me. It is my sincerest hope that as you read this book, you are entertained, but also that you see the correlation between the character's thinking and what manifests in her life. Happy Reading!

PROLOGUE

She'd been separated for over a year and was waiting on the final divorce decree the first time she saw him. She was new to the free dating site, new to dating in general. She was bored, having already finished all of her household chores and errands. She had no one to keep her company but her dog, since her daughter was with her father for the weekend. She'd never initiated a single message on that free dating site, and rarely responded to ones sent to her. She wasn't going to spend one red cent on this waste of time. Then she saw him. Something about his dark eyes caught her attention. The way they held hers from the screen of her laptop computer. He was cute. More than cute…handsome. And she was intrigued by the picture of him with a monkey on his shoulder. Even though it wasn't a full body shot, she could look at his arms and shoulders folded across his chest and see he was in good shape. He had this small smile tugging at the corners of his mouth that said, "Come on, you know you want to send me a message." So, for once, she did. "Hi. Is that a pet monkey, or is this a vacation pic?" was the message that started it all. She didn't really think he'd respond. After all, he was handsome…sexy…and she was just…her. Average at best.

A plethora of childhood memories, involving her being teased and bullied about her large almond-shaped eyes, her proper speech, brains, horseback riding skills (which made her even "whiter" than her speech) were stored in the back of her mind. She didn't think she was cool, or pretty, or interesting…occasionally cute, at best. Nine years married to a man who fell out of love with her, or maybe never even loved her in the first place, framed how she thought of herself. All her failed relationships did. Every one of her relationships ended the same way until she'd met her husband. Things were different for a while, then he'd cheated on her too. They were all cheaters, every single one of them. To make matters worse, she usually found out she was the "other woman," never the first choice; never the one being cheated on, until along came the man who would become her husband. He was arrogant, sure, but he didn't cheat on her. Didn't every woman want a man with confidence? Must be love, right? She was never starry-eyed or crazy about him, but they got along okay and nothing relationship-ending happened, so after two years together, they got married. It seemed like the next logical step.

The proposal was well thought out. He'd tried to get her to go walk to where he'd met her in DC on the National Mall. Only it was December and in the low 20s and windy; she'd had a long day and her feet were killing her. Oh, and the heels on her new boots would get messed up in the gravel, so she declined to go out for a walk. After not speaking to her for an hour in the car, he'd simply handed her the ring. Right there in the car. It certainly wasn't the fairytale proposal she'd dreamt about. But then again, neither was the marriage. About ten months in, she realized she'd made a mistake, but she was pregnant by then. For the next nine years, she discovered how worthless she was to him. How much she didn't matter. How insignificant she was. When the arguments got worse and worse, she stayed. When her hair started falling out in clumps, she stayed. When she cried herself to sleep nightly, she stayed.

She didn't want her daughter to have a broken family. Another statistic. But then, he had cheated on her too. Things became intolerable when he'd publicly berated her and flaunted his affair in front of the family. Finally, she saw that things would only get worse. There was no love, or even friendship...he had no respect for her whatsoever. She realized she had been a fool to hang in there as long as she did and she left.

A year later, she was dealing with becoming a co-parent, a vicious divorce, dry pockets (divorce ain't cheap) and realizing that other than wife, mother, and social worker, she had no idea who she was. She felt transparent...or naked, maybe. Like everyone could see how beneath the surface, she wasn't what she appeared to be. She wasn't really anyone at all.

She certainly didn't think this handsome stranger would even bother to respond. But he did, almost immediately (vacation pic, not a pet monkey). Then he introduced himself and began asking questions about her. She was so nervous and excited her hands kept striking the wrong keys as she typed. They chatted for a while...names, ages, kids, professions, hobbies, a few jokes here and there. He was also separated and could relate to what she was going through. Then he sent her his number and told her to call. She couldn't believe the screen. This had to be like one of the jokes played on her in high school where the guy pretends to like her and then the second she calls, she finds out there's a room full of all the cool kids ready to laugh at the preppy nerd. Some cool guy who'd had a girlfriend all along. Either that or he'd be like all the other Internet guys, attempting to meet somewhere (like a parking lot) to try to arrange a quick screw before the wife at home misses him.

But much to her surprise, they spoke. He didn't ask for pictures of her ass or ask her opinion on oral and anal sex. He didn't send her pictures of his dick. They spoke easily for hours...and this went on for weeks. He'd send her "good morning" and "I hope you're having a great day" messages and he knew the difference

11

between your and you're! Then, one evening, he asked her out to a karaoke bar (was she really going to let this man hear her sing on the first date!?) he knew not too far away. She tore through everything in her closet looking for just the right outfit to wear, finally settling on fitted jeans and a sweater with knee high wedge boots. She called her brother and told her where she was going and gave him the man's name and number, just in case she disappeared. He was already there waiting when she arrived (she'd gotten lost on the way and was late). She recognized him easily from his pictures…God, was he handsome! He greeted her with a warm smile and a friendly hug…and he smelled good, too. They chatted for a while, sharing a basket of Buffalo wings and fries. Then, they began looking for a duet (she must be out of her mind) to sing. Deciding some liquid courage would help, she ordered a vodka and cranberry. And then, still not feeling brave enough, she ordered another. He was keeping pace with her even though the drinks were pretty strong (she'd gone to a white party school…she could hold her liquor) and eventually, they were doing vodka shots and dancing, waiting for their turn to sing their duet.

At some point on the dance floor, she realized that she'd never had more fun with a guy. She didn't feel at all shy or self-conscious. She felt like they were the only two people there. They danced and laughed like they'd known each other forever. During a trip to the crowded restroom, two women stopped her to ask how long she'd been with him. "You two were just made for each other. I can tell these things!" one woman had said. "How long have you been together?" the other woman asked. "It's our first date, but I think I like him," she'd told her. "My God, I'd kill to have a good-looking guy like that look at me the way he's looking at you!" the first woman said. Both women wished her luck and advised her to sleep with him for sure as they parted ways.

She returned to the table, and then they hit the dance floor again. The bar was crowded and they were pretty far down on the waitlist for their chance to sing, thank God. Still talking and laughing, and at this point, singing to each other, getting ready for their duet. Then, she kissed him. She'd never kissed a guy first in her entire life. Ever. But, she just had to. Then the DJ announced that there would be no more karaoke and it was final call. They'd been there for hours, talking and dancing. She couldn't believe how the time had passed so quickly.

Unable to let the evening end, she did something else she'd never done before. The ultimate naughty girl move (in her mind), she slept with him on the first date. Neither of them was in any condition to drive, so they'd walked to a hotel across the parking lot. They kissed (and oh, he was a great kisser) and he began to undress her. He picked her up (did he just pick her up!?) and laid her on the bed. They made love until they fell asleep (or passed out). Although the details got a little fuzzy from all the vodka, to this day, she remembers it as the best date she'd ever had.

After returning home, she halfway expected to never hear from him again. After all, you know what they say about girls who give it up on the first date. But, much to her pleasant surprise, he kept calling and texting. Often, just as she was thinking about him, she'd receive a text or he'd call, like he knew she was thinking about him. And then the day she thought she was waiting for finally arrived. Her divorce papers came in the mail. She was officially divorced. Free to move on. And it scared the shit out of her. This could actually turn into a real relationship. She visualized herself falling in love with him...and then finding out he was cheating on her. Or that he didn't really care and was just passing time or pretending or whatever. She felt the pain in the middle of her chest – the heavy, searing, gaping hole – the one not yet healed from her husband, from her college boyfriends, from her high school boyfriends, from childhood. And she decided she'd never give him the opportunity to add to that pain…She'd rather have the memory of the great guy and the perfect night, so she decided to walk away. She reminded him that his divorce wasn't finalized (as hers hadn't been until the day before) and that he wasn't as far along in the process as she had been. After all, he might decide to reconcile with his wife. She flat out asked him, "What if I fall in love with you?" He replied that he would love her back. "How do you know that? How could you possibly know that?" She challenged him. He told her to trust him. Asked her to give it a try.

He'd love her back? Ha! Who had? How could she believe him? How could she trust him? He was self-confident and good looking and talented and she was…her. How could he love her? She decided he couldn't and wouldn't…so she walked away.

CHAPTER 1

"You're late again, Desi. Meeting starts in 5 minutes," my boss said as I came rushing through the door, computer bag over one shoulder, arm full of files, coffee in the free hand. Does he think I don't know that? Like I'm just running through the door like a plate twirler in the circus for fun?

"Sorry Ted, I got halfway here and realized my daughter left her lunch in the back seat. Field trip today. I had to run back to the school." It seemed like that was always the way it went on mornings when I was running just a little late. Something else would happen to make me even later. Traffic, sick kid, sick dog, flat tire, asteroid crashing into the Earth. Always something. I'd never been the world's most punctual person, but since my husband (ex-husband, actually) and I had split up, getting everything done by myself as a single mom…let's just say the struggle has been real.

I'm a case manager for child protective services. I go to homes and evaluate the safety of children. I also do custody evaluations. Once a week, I meet with my supervisor, Ted, and sometimes a team of other investigators to make sure everyone is on the same page, current on paperwork, and ready for court when necessary, which was fairly often. This latest case for custody evaluation was both sad and humorous at the same time.

"It's okay, Desi, I know you're trying," Ted said with a sympathetic look. "I have court in an hour and a half, so let's get started." He was a good guy. Married with five kids ages 17 years to 18 months. I'd worked with him for seven years now, so he knew my work ethic and that my heart truly was with every one of those children I interviewed. He also knew the hell I'd gone through with my separation, divorce, and my very own ridiculous custody battle. My own coworkers had to interview me. Investigate my home. It took a while to get over the feelings of nakedness…the violation of having my coworkers forced to turn a critical eye on my life. Maia, my eleven-year-old daughter, is everything to me.

My ex-husband, Maurice Kane, told me he'd make me sorry for leaving him when I discovered his affair with some Instagram model who worked at Carl Jr.'s at the mall. She'd posted a picture of the two of them on a beach, and somehow a friend of a friend saw it and it eventually made its way to me. We hadn't been getting along for quite some time, but to know I was putting in all of this effort to make the marriage work, doing little things to show I cared, and he was committing the same ultimate betrayal as every other man had done. The one thing he swore would never happen. He promised me he'd be different from the rest. I packed an overnight bag and walked out the door with nothing else but Maia. About a month later, I wavered and even considered getting back with him. He was initially sweet and apologetic. He suggested counseling, sent flowers to my job, and called regularly to apologize and remind me he loved me. But when a month passed and I still hadn't forgiven him or moved back in, he showed up to my nephew's graduation with the Instagram model on his arm. Up until that point, our separation had been relatively quiet. I wasn't sure if I wanted to go through with the divorce. I didn't want to take Maia away from her father or rob her of the experience of growing up in a two-parent home. Maurice chose the most public way to show the entire family how our marriage was truly over.

"Tell me about Breanna Lee," Ted said as I walked into his office.

Byron Lee and Sarita Lawrence both wanted sole custody of their daughter, Breanna. So did Breanna's aunt, Corinne Moon. Neither of the parents worked and most of the time, she stayed with her aunt and cousins. Ms. Moon took care of homework, hair, feeding, clothing and pretty much all of her care.

"Ms. Lawrence is 23 years old, unemployed and seems to be pretty happy about it. She stays in a row house on Tulip Lane," I began, looking down at my notes. Over the years, I'd developed my own version of shorthand. I was probably the only person who could decipher my notes.

The narrow house had been filthy, which really says a lot when you consider that this visit had been scheduled for a month. Most of the time, when people know they have social services on the way, they clean up. Not Serita Lawrence. Dirty dishes were growing mold in the sink. Roaches scattered every time we walked into a room. Garbage bags had crudely been taped over the windows. The smell of cigarette smoke hung so thickly in the air, you could almost cut it with a knife. A bare, stained mattress and a cheap lamp made up the room Breanna stayed in when she was with mom. This was clearly no place for Breanna.

Ms. Lawrence chain-smoked the entire time I interviewed her. She hadn't bothered to change out of her pajamas or even to bathe. She was wearing what probably used to be a pink fuzzy robe, but was now dirty and matted and faded. She had a grease stained bonnet covering her waist length weave and her fake eyelashes were almost long enough to reach the middle of her forehead. Between puffs of smoke, she told me, "Yeah, I love my daughter. She always eat when she here. Why should he get to claim her on his taxes? He don't do shit but drink, smoke weed, and sell drugs anyway. He ain't shit."

The day I met Mr. Lee would go down in the books as the most interesting interview I've ever had.

"Lawd have mercy! You is beautiful! Mmm-mmm-mmm." Mr. Lee exclaimed, rubbing his palms together and licking his lips when I'd arrived at the house.

"Good afternoon, Mr. Lee, I'm Desiree Kane with Social Services. I'm here to conduct the court ordered custody evaluation. May I come in?"

It's not like I've never been hit on at work before, because it happens every once-in-a-while. Well, maybe more than once-in-a-while. I'm five-foot-four and in decent shape. I wear between a size six and an eight, or a ten if it's slim cut (somehow, the waist on the eight is always too big, but the hips and rear in the six are too small...struggle of a black woman with hips and ass). I get asked out to dinner from time to time.

Mr. Lee had to be 120 pounds soaking wet and was probably five-foot-six. You'd think his name was "Terrence" since it was tattooed down the side of his face. I looked at the paperwork quickly. His middle name was Harold. Byron Harold Lee. So who was Terrence?

He had a "G" tattooed right in the middle of his forehead, and enough tears to be sobbing tattooed from his eyes down the side of his face. The t-shirt he was wearing allowed me to see that he had a smoking gun tattooed on one side of his neck, and on the other a set of blue lips and the Scorpio zodiac sign.

"Please do, Miss Lady. It is a pleasure to have you in my home." He reached for my hand with a graphically illustrated one of his own, and when I shook it, he pulled my hand toward his and tried to kiss it.

"Thank you." I said stiffly as I quickly yanked my hand away before he could get it to his lips. "Let's start with a tour of the home." I said in my stiffest professional voice. He smiled and seemed undeterred.

He led the way inside. I was shocked at the stark contrast to Ms. Lawrence's home. This place was immaculate. The gleaming hardwood floors were clean swept and it smelled like lemon Pledge in the house. There was a plush, chocolate brown leather living room set facing a large entertainment center with a built-in fireplace that boasted a huge TV, an Xbox One, a Wii U, and a PlayStation 4. There was a huge stereo system against the wall. The dining room had a beautifully carved mahogany table and buffet against the wall with a large, fancy gold mirror above it. There were several paintings on the walls. State of the art appliances were in the kitchen. All the rooms had beautiful, expensive furniture. Clearly, all the things in this house cost a small fortune...which is suspicious when you're 25 years old with no job. His place was nicer than mine and I'm 35 years old with a career I've had for twelve years. It certainly appeared that Ms. Lawrence might have been telling the truth about him dealing drugs.

"I was drunk and high when I got her mother pregnant. Wish I'd never gone to that party," Mr. Lee began as we entered the living room. I'd chosen the armchair across from the couch where he sat down. "I was so messed up, I barely even remember being with her. That's probably a good thing. I can't even lie about that. She's horrible. Don't even want to wash her ass in the morning. I tried to do right by her and let her stay with me while she was pregnant. My baby can stay with me and have whatever she wants. Her mother's house is just nasty. Mice don't even want to go in there. Just big ass rats. My baby don't need to be in a place like that ever." And on this one point, I couldn't have agreed with him more.

"Ms. Lady, can I ask you a question?" He leaned forward, his hazel eyes twinkling as he began rubbing his palms together and licking his lips again. "Do you have pretty feet? I can't tell with them boots you got on. They is fly, though. I like a woman that can walk in heels. And I love a woman with pretty feet." I froze and took a mental moment to come up with a response, because my first response probably would have gotten me fired. He looked me up and down like he was a starving man staring at a steak dinner and continued rubbing his palms together.

"Mr. Lee," I began sternly. "I'm here to conduct a custody investigation and make a recommendation to the court regarding custody of your daughter, Breanna. I'm not here on a social visit or to flirt. I'd like to keep this as brief and professional as possible. Do you think you could help me with that?"

He smiled as if I'd just told him a dirty joke. "I like how you call me Mr. Lee," he said, eyes still twinkling and clearly unaffected by what I'd just said to him.

"It's your name, sir. You may call me Ms. Kane," I said. What else could I possibly say to get this interview back on track and end his flirting? I just decided to ignore it and move on. "What's your occupation?" I left off the "Mr. Lee" since it seemed to get him going.

"Well, Ms. Lady...Oops! I mean, Ms. Kane, I am currently unemployed." He said with a smile.

"When is the last time you were employed?" I asked. I had my pen and pad ready to take down some notes on his work history.

"I've never been employed, unless you want to count shoveling snow for my grandmother." Well, that certainly made the note taking easy. He was looking at me with a slight smile on his face. I also got the sense that he was gauging my reaction.

"This is a very nice house. How do you afford it?" I asked as if I hadn't figured it out. There was always the possibility it belonged to a family member or had been left to him, but I was pretty certain this wasn't the case.

"I have connections. I do favors for them, they do favors for me." He said evasively. And who is them? I froze for a second, trying to think of how to frame my next question. He saved me the trouble.

"Look, Ms. Kane," he began earnestly. All signs of flirtation were suddenly gone. "I know you not stupid. You see all this fly shit here." He gestured around his home. It was, indeed, fly. "You know I don't have a legal nine-to-five. And I know you seen the rat trap her mother lives in. You wasn't going to recommend either of us custody anyway, I hope. I love my baby with all my heart, but I ain't no good for her. Go on and recommend her auntie gets custody. I'll make sure she's got all the money she needs to take care of her. We don't even need to finish this interview. I just wanted to make sure her mother didn't get custody."

I just blinked for a few seconds. "Well, then I guess we're done here. Thank you for your time, Mr. Lee. I'll interview her aunt and then make my recommendation to the court."

As I stood to leave, he stopped me. The twinkle was back in his eyes. "Now that all that unpleasant business is taken care of...how about you let me buy you dinner?"

* * * * *

Ted wiped the tears from his eyes, laughing at my recap of Mr. Lee. "He's quite a character."

"It's not funny!" I laughed. Who was I kidding? The dude was hysterical.

"Okay, back to business. Did you interview the aunt?" Ted asked, trying to pull himself together.

"Yes, and I interviewed Breanna as well," I told him, looking through my reports. "The aunt is a nurse. Ms. Lawrence's older sister. Her son, Adam, is 19 and goes to the local community college. He helps out and even goes to parent-teacher meetings if Ms. Moon has to work a late shift. Breanna wants to stay with them, and pretty much does anyway. According to her teacher, she's reading above grade level and is a pleasure to teach, unless she's been to her mother's house, then she's rude and disrespectful to the other children for about a week after the visit."

"Did the teacher mention how she behaved following visits to her father's house?" Ted asked.

"She said she still arrived on time and with her homework done. The teacher's only complaint was that Mr. Lee kept asking about her feet." I tried my hardest to keep a straight face, but we both dissolved into a fit of laughter again.

CHAPTER 2

Three years had gone by, but I still thought of him. Spencer Thomas. I got a tin gle in my spine…hell, I got a tingle all over when I thought of him. It was almost like a dream. One perfect night. Sometimes I dreamed I was back on that date again. In his arms as he pulled me closer…Somehow, someway, Spencer would just cross my mind and linger. I'd remember how amazing I felt that night. I wondered what we would be if I hadn't pushed him away. Would we be best friends or lovers? Maybe we'd be married with children. Probably angry at each other and not speaking…the relationship long over-with.

Sometimes, I wondered if he ever thought of me. Probably not. An amazing guy like that…probably had amazing dates all the time. It was probably only special to me. And after 3 years…he probably didn't even remember me.

I snapped out of my reverie. I was in a new relationship now, and we'd been relatively happy, I guess. He was nice enough… had a job and his own house. The sex was pretty good. He was handsome and in fantastic shape. Jarod Kelly was about to pick me up so we could go out to dinner and a movie. We'd been dating for about eight months now. He was a welder, building bomb-proof containers for detonating bombs inside of, or something like that. He said the company he worked for was small but highly specialized. After he finished these gigantic containers, they were shipped to Israel. He was a little rough around the edges, but smart and funny. He seemed like he made good money. I never asked, but he never seemed to be broke. Maia loved him and was always excited to see him. So if nothing in particular was wrong, then I guess everything was alright…right?

This was an area I struggled with in relationships. How do you know when you've found the one? How do you know when it's right? How do you know how hard to try before giving someone up? "You know when you know." "When you find the one who completes you." I'd heard those clichés my whole life, but the bottom line was, I'd never once known. No one had ever "completed" me. I always tried to be the perfect girlfriend (or wife), yet I always seemed to get blindsided. And it got worse every time. I didn't even want to think about the one I'd dated before Jarod… What a waste of time he turned out to be. And time was a precious commodity at my age. I was in my mid-thirties now. I figure I have limited shelf life remaining. I needed to find the right one while my bits and pieces were all where they were supposed to be. I couldn't think of a worse fate than being on the dating scene in my fifties. Who would want me? Who would fall in love with me then? It was bad enough I had a c-section scar and breasts that had clearly nursed a fat, healthy baby. I mean, I know I'm in better shape than a lot of women my age, but I certainly didn't have the body I had at 23!

My cell rang. I glanced at the screen and rolled my eyes. My ex-husband. He should have been here hours ago to pick up our daughter. "Hello?" Why do we do that? Say "hello?" like we don't know who's on the other end. It pops right up on the screen, after all.

"Hey," Maurice said. "I can't come get Maia until later. Something came up."

"You were supposed to pick her up two hours ago. You couldn't have called sooner? I have plans," I said with irritation in my voice.

"Oh, are you dating now?" Maurice asked. His voice indicated a more than casual interest.

"How is that any of your business? Do I ask you about your personal life?" We had a bitter divorce and an even more bitter custody battle. Even though he married the Instagram model and she was pregnant with his second child, he clearly hadn't let go of the malice he felt towards me. I always kept our conversations as brief as possible.

"You know, I know about him, right? Maia told me," he said smugly.

His attitude irritated me. It's not like I was trying to keep my relationship with Jarod a secret, it just wasn't any of his business. "Okay. What's your point?"

"You're finally trying to get over me, huh?" his voice was so smug, I wished I could smack him through the phone. "Finally decided you needed to get some? Hope he's as good as I was."

"Mo, I was over you before I walked out the door. I hate to burst your bubble, but time and experience have shown me you weren't hard to replace – emotionally, mentally and especially sexually. I hadn't been with many men before we got married. Now I know you have no clue what you're doing. Had I slept around when I was younger, we never would have gotten married. When should I drop Maia off?" Why had I gotten into it with him? He just irritates me so badly, sometimes my temper gets the better of me. Every word I said was true, but I generally tried to take the high road. Today, I just didn't feel like it.

"You know what, I'll be there in an hour," he said, and just hung up.

* * * * *

"Maia, your dad's on his way. Did you remember to pack your charger?" I asked. She'd been asking for a phone for two years, and I'd finally caved and gotten her one for her eleventh birthday a few months ago.

"Yes, Mom," she said, sounding exasperated. How do kids do that? Make the word "yes" into three syllables.

"Um…What's with the attitude, Missy? It was just a question. Last time you forgot it and you almost died not being able to use your phone for a whole day. I'm just trying to spare you some pain and suffering," I reminded her.

"Mom…do I *really* have to go?" She asked me for the umteenth time. She turned and looked at me with her deep chocolate brown eyes. My eyes. She looked so much like her father, especially when she was serious, but the eyes were all me. She'd lost all of the baby fat and was all legs now. She even had little buds coming up under her shirt. Where did my cute little ladybug go? This was a young woman. She was so beautiful.

"Yes, Sweetie. You do. He's your father and he loves you. As much as I miss you when you're gone, it wouldn't be fair for me to keep you all of the time. You have two parents, not one."

Maia wasn't fond of Cherrie, her new stepmother. She was 22 years old and from what I'd seen, she hadn't spent too much time around kids. She was incredibly awkward around Maia. Once, I heard her ask Maia if she wanted to watch Yo Gabba Gabba. Maia looked at her as if she had two heads and told her she hadn't watched that since she was four. Hopefully she was a fast learner, because she was due any day now.

"She doesn't like me," Maia told me flatly.

"I don't think that's true. She just doesn't know you well enough and she has no experience with kids. Give her a chance. You just might find you like her."

"She acts more like a kid than I do, Mom. She whines and pouts at Dad all the time! What grown woman does that!? I don't even do that, and I'm eleven!" Maia exclaimed, looking completely disgusted.

I had to hide a smile. Although I completely agreed with her, the bottom line was that I wanted her to have two parents and she was going to see her father this weekend.

"Try to have a good time. Spend some time with your dad," I said, ending the discussion. I wrapped her in a hug and kissed the top of her head. She was getting so tall.

"Okay," she said glumly, hugging me back. Her phone buzzed just then. Text message. "It's Dad," she said as she grabbed her bag and began walking toward the front door. "He says for me to wait on the porch because he's in a hurry." I stepped out on the porch to wait with her.

"I'll pop popcorn and we'll lay in my bed and watch Ferris Bueller when you get back on Sunday. And we can do each other's nails, okay?" She'd discovered Ferris Bueller about a month ago and fell in love with the movie. The classics never get old. Maybe I'd have her watch Willow next time we did a girls' night. I loved that movie as a child.

"Okay," she smiled. "Love you, Mom."

She gave me a quick peck and then headed down the driveway when she saw her father's car turn onto to the street. I hoped she and her father could find some common ground. Although he'd remained in her life, Maurice seemed to have a really hard time relating to Maia, and now that he had a child bride with a baby on the way, things had only gotten worse. I had no idea how to fix it. I sighed and headed inside to finish getting ready.

When I got separated and then divorced, I felt like my whole world was going to collapse in on itself. In the beginning, when it was his time with Maia, I thought I would die. There were days when I wouldn't even get out of bed. I just wanted the bed to swallow me into some deep abyss. I had to work hard to find the pieces and patch them together. To make myself appear whole. To be almost okay. As much as I wanted to be in love and to be loved and married and maybe even have another baby, I was terrified of the hurt that follows failed relationships. The older I got, the more it hurt and the more I had to lose.

CHAPTER 3

"You look beautiful tonight, Baby," Jarod told me as we walked into the movie theater.

"Awww, thanks, Jarod," I beamed at him. Do guys really mean that, or is it just something they have to say on a date? Kinda like saying "God bless you" when someone sneezes…

"You're welcome," he replied, kissing my hand. The look he gave me sent a little shiver down my spine. He was a good-looking man with polished bronze skin and long eyelashes. He had full lips and a great smile, which were framed by the neatest goatee I'd ever seen. He always wore his shirts fitted, none of that baggy stuff. He probably wanted everyone to see his broad chest and shoulders. I certainly didn't mind looking.

"You look great, too," I told him. Then added, "but you always do."

"I have to make sure I look like I belong with you," he told me. "Just trying to keep up with your beauty."

The restaurant was a little crowded for a Thursday night. Ordinarily, we didn't bother with reservations because we never had too much of a wait. Tonight, it appeared that was a mistake. We spent the wait looking at the menu, so when we're seated after fifteen minutes, we were ready to order.

"I hit the jackpot when I met you," Jarod said after we'd been seated and ordered the food. "A beautiful woman who's into comic book superheroes? That's just…sexy. The cosplay could be amazing. I'll be Batman and you can be Catwoman. I'd love to see you dressed as Catwoman." He looked at me with a devilish twinkle in his eye.

"In middle school, it just made me a bigger nerd. I never thought it would be a turn-on someday," I said with a laugh.

"Well, now you know. Now, we just have to get you converted. I can't believe you think with Batman's intelligence, he'd be defeated by Superman!" He shook his head in amazement.

"I think it depends on the type of battle. If Batman had time to prepare, sure, he'd invent some great gadgets using Kryptonite… probably encase it in lead as a shield…Superman might have a hard time beating him. But head on, if they just met and fought, Superman would obliterate Batman! Laser eyes! Boom, Batman's done." It seemed like simple math to me.

"He wouldn't be done. He'd think of something," Jarod stubbornly said.

"If Superman wanted him dead, he'd be dead," I said with a laugh.

"We'll see how it goes down in the movie," Jarod said. We were going to see Batman Vs. Superman after dinner.

"I'm just saying, Bruce Wayne is a human, like you or me. No matter how smart we are, head on, what are we going to do to Superman?" I was enjoying our little debate. Maia wasn't into comic book heroes and I hadn't had too many opportunities to talk strengths and weaknesses of superheroes in years.

"Lex Luther is his greatest nemesis. What's super about him?" Jarod countered.

"You know, they're both good guys. I wonder what they're even fighting about," I mused. I was excited about the movie either way. I was sure we'd have plenty to talk about afterwards.

We had relatively slow service at the restaurant, so we were a little pressed for time to catch the 9:20 showing. It was already 9:10 and we hadn't picked up the tickets or gotten refreshments yet. There was a long line at the ticket booth, but there were several open kiosks.

I'm so glad most movie theaters had the kiosks now. It used to take forever to wait on the tickets. We had ours within two minutes of entering the theater.

"Why don't you get the popcorn and I'll find us some seats," he said, handing me my ticket. "Hopefully we can still get good seats."

"Sure," I said, and began walking over to the concessions area. Of course, the lines were all fairly long. There were about six or seven people ahead of me.

As I stood in line, I began to let my mind wander. Actually, "let" is a generous term. My mind tends to wander where it wants whenever it's given free reign to do so. It was such a lovely March day. Warm, but not hot and not a cloud in the sky. I wish I could have gotten out to ride my friend Judy's horse, Ichabod. Icky was a retired thoroughbred show horse, which put us at right about at the same speed. I used to ride in lots of horse shows in high school and college, but once real life came knocking, time and money for horse shows went by the wayside. Even though I didn't ride in shows anymore, I still love to ride whenever I have the free time and money. It's one of the few times my mind easily relaxes and just focuses on what I'm doing. Today would have been perfect. I could almost feel the wind on my face. Something about the bond between me and the horse...

"Excuse me, miss?" a deep male voice behind me jerked me out of my daydream.

"Me?" I asked, turning around. He was a tall, dark piece of chocolate with a neatly trimmed goatee and gleaming white teeth...Damn, this brother was fine. His locks came to the middle of his back and were freshly twisted and pulled back from his face, revealing a precisely trimmed beard line. And he smelled oh so good.

"I've been back here trying to respectfully admire the view, and curiosity got the best of me. I love a woman with natural hair. I just had to see your face," he said with a smile.

"Oh, well I hope you weren't too disappointed," I laughed. I wasn't sure what else to say, so I began to turn around. I have never been good at accepting compliments about my appearance. I mean, I know I'm not ugly, but I don't see anything spectacular or out of the ordinary other than my huge eyes. It always made me uncomfortable when people spoke about my appearance, especially strangers. Especially good looking, well-muscled, sexy strangers.

"Oh no, not at all. You are absolutely breathtaking. My name is Jason," he said, extending his hand.

"Desiree," I said, shaking his hand.

"A beautiful name to go with a beautiful queen," he smiled. "Please tell me I'm lucky enough that you're here alone."

"Sorry, I'm here with my boyfriend. He just went to get the seats. I hope you enjoy your movie," I said as I turned around to order the popcorn.

"You too, Queen," Jason smiled. "He's a lucky man. You're a beautiful woman."

"You're very sweet," I said as I paid and began walking toward the theater. I refused to look back, but I could feel his eyes watching me walk away. I stopped at the condiment station to get a little butter for the popcorn and lots of napkins before heading down the hall to the theater. It's always a nice ego boost when I get hit on, and this good-looking brother had me feeling like a runway model. A really short one, though. But no matter how many times (not that it happened all the time) I was hit on, I never gave out my number. I remembered all my past relationships and discovering how I wasn't my partner's first option. I never wanted to make anyone feel that way, so I never did the side-dude/side-chick thing.

I took a second to let my eyes adjust to the darkness before I began looking for Jarod. I spotted him waving in the middle of the crowded theater and "excuse me'd" my way over to the empty seat beside him.

"You sure took long enough," he whispered irritably. "You missed all the trailers."

"I had to get the popcorn. The line was long," I reminded him. Maybe he'd forgotten what the line looked like. The opening credits were still rolling. I hadn't missed anything. I settled in and took a handful of popcorn out of the bag. I usually pop my own popcorn at home and use real butter. It was so much better than the theater popcorn with their fake butter oil, but somehow it just didn't feel right to watch the movie without my bag of popcorn and a Sprite.

"Uh-huh. So did you give him your number?" he hissed in my ear. He sounded angry and smug all at the same time. Certainly not like he had earlier when he was complimenting my beauty.

"Who?" I asked, genuinely puzzled.

"I saw you flirting with the tall guy with the dreads. I came to see what was taking you so long and there you two were, looking real cozy."

I just looked at him. I was friendly, sure, that's my nature, but I certainly wasn't flirting. And how does one look cozy standing in line without even touching?

"So when are the two of you meeting up?" he persisted.

"I told him I had a boyfriend and we parted ways. It was nothing to get all upset over," I told him. "Let's just watch the movie."

"Yeah, alright," he said grumpily.

We watched the rest of the movie in silence. We're normally not gabby during movies, but this silence felt…cold. No whispered comments. No smiles exchanged. He didn't react to any of the of the movie, which had some pretty entertaining scenes. He just stared at the screen and slowly chewed on popcorn. Was he really that worried about some guy in line? Jarod was a good-looking guy. I'm sure he'd had women approach him before. I trusted him to say he was in a relationship. Clearly, the feeling wasn't mutual.

CHAPTER 4

As we rode home, Jarod was just as quiet as he was in the movie theater. I was content to let him sit in silence. I'm not into bickering, or whooping and hollering. Fighting was just not my thing. Sure, I can make some smart remarks if I'm pushed, but I'm a lover, not a fighter. I'd developed a pretty healthy amount of sarcasm as a defense mechanism in middle school. I was picked on and bullied terribly, but I knew if I ever got into a fight, my parents would have killed me, regardless of who started it. In kindergarten, a girl threw sand in my face when we were playing in the sandbox. It got in my hair (mom had just cornrowed it, so I was already going to be in trouble for that one), mouth and eyes. Without missing a beat, I'd hurled a fistful of sand back into her face. She screamed as the sand got in her eyes and the teacher came running over to see what was wrong. We both had to sit in timeout and our parents were informed of the incident. My mother lectured me for twenty minutes before paddling my legs with the wooden cooking spoon, and then lecturing me again.

Didn't I know I could have scratched her eyes and caused blindness? Why didn't I tell the teacher? What gave me the right to hurt someone else? "What about *my* eyes?" I asked. "She could have done that to me to. And we weren't arguing or playing. She just threw sand in my face for no reason!" The response had been that I was fine and I didn't have the right to harm someone else on purpose. We then read Bible verses about vengeance and anger. I guess I internalized that experience and decided it was better to be bullied at school than to get in trouble for fighting back. If Jarod wanted to be an asshole and stew in his bad mood, he could do it by himself. I wasn't participating.

As I sat in Jarod's Altima staring out the passenger window, my mind drifted to Maia. I wondered if she was enjoying her time with her father and stepmother. She was turning into such a mature young lady. She had a swim meet coming up next weekend. She always loved the water. I took one of those water baby classes at the local recreation center when she was a baby. The water was freezing. My teeth began to chatter just thinking about those frigid classes. But Maia had loved it and…

"So, when are the two of you getting together?" Jarod asked suddenly, breaking my train of thought.

"What? Who?" I asked, turning to face him. I'd been lost in my own world. I'd almost forgotten he was there. As if I was having a silent cab ride home. Had I missed some part of this conversation? He was silent up until this moment and then asked the question so conversationally.

"Don't play dumb. You and your new boyfriend," he smirked. Surely he was joking. But as I looked at his face, I could see there wasn't a hint of laughter or levity in him. His voice was angry and cold. I could see his jaw working as he was grinding his teeth. His hands were tightly gripping the steering wheel.

"Are you seriously still on this? Don't you think you're being a little dramatic? Is all this really necessary? The man complimented me. I thanked him. He asked if I was single and I said 'No' and told him you were waiting for me. Why is that such a big deal to you?" It seemed pretty simple to me.

"So you say. How do I know that's all that happened? Women these days are slick. Maybe you were happy to get the attention."

He took his eyes off of the road to glare at me. I was tired and really irritated at this point. I don't get many evenings out, and for this to be how I spent my night...I'd put on all kinds of lacy contraptions under my jeans and sweater. I had planned on an evening of passion. Something I'd be able to fantasize about until the next time I had a free weekend with no work and no Maia. I usually treasured this time to myself. I certainly wished I was home alone now. Maybe with a glass of wine. Maybe I should have had a girls' night out. This evening was certainly a bust.

"I guess you'll just have to trust me," I said flatly. I was truly feeling over the whole incident. If you could even call it an incident. Nothing had happened. I had done absolutely nothing wrong or disrespectful to our relationship, but somehow it had still cost me my entire evening. I was feeling especially grumpy because my boy-shorts had decided to wander uncomfortably north...I certainly wasn't close enough to Jarod to pull that wedgie. It just added to my mounting irritation.

"Trust has to be earned," he informed me in a tone nearly identical to the one my father used to use when he lectured me as a teenager.

"We've been together for eight months. What reason have I ever given you to not trust me?" I hadn't been with anyone else or even talked to anyone else for that matter. I wasn't on any dating sites anymore and if any past interests did call, I'd quickly cut them off to tell them I was in a relationship.

"Anybody can fake it that long. Maybe you've been playing a role all along. Maybe you two made plans to get together later. I'd never know, right?" Although I didn't like to argue, I could feel myself getting more and more upset. I could feel the irritation begin to change into anger. I finally let go of the last of my hopes for turning this evening around and began to prepare for war instead.

"Is that really what you think of me?" Cue righteous indignation.

"It's not about what I think of you. It's what I know women are capable of," he countered practically.

"Everyone's capable of cheating. Yourself included. Doesn't mean they do it," I said flatly.

"Right. So how do I know that you chose not to do it?" he asked, sounding like a state prosecutor.

"Well, when you put it that way, I guess you don't. I'd have thought you know me a little better than that by now, but I guess I was wrong." Turn the indignation up a notch or two. I always answer his calls when I'm available, and if I'm not, I text and let him know I'll call him. I check up on him. On top of that, I spend most of my child-free nights with him.

"I'm just saying, what's to stop you from getting a quick fuck in. I'd never know. It didn't take too many dates before you slept with me. Maybe you like strange dick. Maybe I'm getting boring."

And that was what did it. My lips pursed and my entire attitude shifted. Earlier, I wanted to put his mind at ease and move on. Now…I was ready for some verbal sparring. I guess this is how the relationship with Jarod was going to end – over absolute stupidity.

"So what are you saying?" I challenged, sitting stiffly in the leather bucket seat.

"I'm saying it wasn't hard for me to fuck you. Who else doesn't have to try too hard?" He was still speaking casually, but the way I could see him grinding his teeth ever so slightly gave away that he wasn't as calm as he appeared.

I was absolutely speechless for a few seconds. And livid. I felt heat rush from my hands, up my arms and through the back of my neck. I felt my nostrils flair.

"Try as hard as you can tonight, asshole. I'd sooner fuck a stray cat," I seethed.

Jarod and I had met in the grocery store. Just a chance meeting in the produce section. He was feeling cantaloupes, and I took a moment to admire the view from behind. He was wearing his gym clothes and it was clear he worked out frequently. He turned around and caught me staring. I tried to shrug it off by looking at some tomatoes, but he approached me. "I think you're beautiful and I'd like to find out more about you," he told me, "but I'm just coming from the gym and I don't' want to offend you by standing here for too long. I'm Jarod and I'd like to call you sometime."

I wasn't used to such a straightforward approach. I definitely liked it and I gave him a business card from the case I always kept in my purse. He called me later that night and we ended up talking on the phone for three hours. He was funny and seemed sincere. We talked about everything from religion to politics to sex to grandma's cornbread recipes. I've never felt like a specific number of meetings decides how well you know a person or how much you're feeling a guy.

I've gone out with guys five or six times and still felt like I didn't have a general sense of who they were. Other guys, you get a familiar kind of feeling, like you've met before or can relate to each other in some way. I had already done the whole wait-until-marriage (or at least until you were with the person you were going to marry) bit before and it clearly hadn't gone well. So I didn't feel like I was bound by faith or tradition anymore. We spoke about that at some point during that long call, and he agreed and said he didn't feel you could measure the character of a person by how fast or slowly they decided to have sex, especially in your mid-thirties to early forties. He felt that in many ways, a date limit was like long-term prostitution.

"So…all that shit you said about not judging and feeling the vibe and not believing in a date limit…it was all bullshit and you've been thinking I'm a whore all this time because we didn't wait for five dates or thirty days or whatever?"

"Those are your words, not mine." He held his hands up defensively, like I was about to attack him.

"Fine. Use your words. What are you saying, Jarod?" I crossed my arms over my chest and waited. You know when you're in the heat of an argument and you already know whatever he's going to say next is going to push things to the next level? We were there. I was fully prepared for the next statement to be some sort of asinine statement to which I would have to respond with my squint-faced "What!?" He didn't disappoint.

"I'm just saying you like sex and you're good at it."

I did the whole "what" thing. I really was blown. What was that supposed to mean? So I added "And why on God's green Earth would that ever be a bad thing? Especially for you? You're the one who reaps the benefits!"

"I'm just saying. You had to practice at some point. Maybe you like practicing?" He spoke as if it was practical to think I'd have to be sleeping with multiple men because I was good in bed.

"What's that supposed to mean? I have no self-control and I have to have sex with every man who shows me a little attention because I'm good at it?" I exclaimed incredulously.

"You had to learn it somewhere," he said simply. Like that was supposed to explain everything. Knowing I had a child and an ex-husband, he couldn't have thought I was a virgin when we met.

"So what does that mean? You think I'm some kind of slut?" I was offended and ready to invest in this argument at this point. Clearly it was time to walk away. Might as well make it memorable.

"I didn't say that," he said with a rise in his voice.

"Then what *did* you say?" I asked acidly.

"I'm just saying it's possible that someone who likes sex will have it with someone else."

"And all this time, that's what you've been thinking of me?"

"I don't trust people easily. My past doesn't allow it. I've been screwed over before. I just don't want it to happen again."

This diffused me a little. Like, from terror threat alert red down to orange. I can understand not wanting to be hurt. I've been hurt too, but I hadn't done anything to hurt him. The way he was acting was totally uncalled for.

"I've been hurt before, too. That doesn't mean you get to take it out on me anymore than I can put my past on you. All I did was tell the man I had a boyfriend and you're treating me like I'm cheating on you," I said, folding my arms and turning to look out the window again. We were just about to turn onto my street and I was ready for this evening to end.

"I'm sorry," he said as he turned into my driveway and switched off the ignition. "I saw that man talking to you and you looked so beautiful and then you smiled at him. I thought maybe you were interested in him."

"Yeah? Well I wasn't," I said flatly. "Goodnight," I said as I reached for the door handle.

"Wait," Jarod said, reaching out to grab my hand. "I said I was sorry. Let's go inside and have a drink. Maybe I can give you a massage," he suggested.

"No thanks," I said. "I'm tired and I think I need a little space." I gently pulled my hand away and got out of the car. He got out, too and began walking me to the door.

"Can we talk about this?" he asked.

"I thought we just did," I said as I unlocked the door.

"You know, you're really sexy when you're mad." His voice was like melting chocolate, and any other night, it would have put a sexy smile on my face and had my belly doing flips. He reached for my hand with a salacious smile on his face. I had planned on getting some tonight, especially since Maia was with her father. I'd even worn black and red lacy boy-shorts with a matching demi cup bra, but at this point, I wasn't having it. I was in battle mode. If he said the sky was blue, I'd call it green. Having sex was the last thing on my mind now. "C'mon, Desi, don't be like that," he said to my stone-faced reaction.

"Be like what? A flirtatious whore addicted to sex?" I pulled my hand away. Who the hell did he think he was? How dare he start this whole thing and then call me "baby" and try to be all sweet and sexy. It just made me angrier.

"Desi, that is not what I said. You're blowing this whole thing out of proportion," he said exasperatedly.

"*I'm* blowing this out of proportion? Says the man who started this whole thing because a man showed interest in me and I told him that I was already in a relationship. I wasn't sure you understood the concept of 'proportion' until just now." I opened the door. Don't tell me about blowing anything out of proportion. I'm not sure how you thought this evening would go when you decided to behave like an ass fresh outta high school, but just so you know, this is the result. I'll see myself in. Goodnight." And with that, I went in the house and closed the door.

I could hear him on the other side calling my name. "Desi! Come on, baby, open the door. You're being ridiculous."

I turned back, opened the door and said, "I got your ridiculous right here!" I gave him the finger and then slammed the door in his face. Was it immature? Of course. Did it make me feel better? Oh, yeah.

CHAPTER 5

"Good morning, Ted," I said as I walked into the office. I'd been on time all week and was feeling pretty proud of myself.

"Four days in a row. You must be trying to set some sort of record," he said with a smile.

That was about all of the time I had for small talk. I had four reports I needed to get typed and filed before the day was out. I had a court date the next day about Breanna Lee. Maia's science fair project was taking up so much of our time in addition to the upcoming swim meets. I was on time to work all week because I'd been getting up at four in the morning to get work done around the house. Laundry, prepping meals in the crock pot because we had swim practice and swim meets in addition to the project. She also had dance lessons twice a week. She was also asking for violin lessons, which would make the week's schedule even crazier. I usually had enough time to pick her up, scarf down whatever I put in the slow cooker that morning, change clothes and then head out to whatever practice or game it was for the evening. I was exhausted. I didn't even have the energy to think about making up with Jarod. And I wasn't entirely sure I wanted to. I actually fell asleep holding the phone when he called last night.

"Hey, baby, I've been missing you," he said.

"Oh?" Was all I replied before yawning. I missed him a little, I guess. It was nice when he slept over on the nights Maia stayed with her father. Certainly better than sleeping alone. But I wasn't going to tell him that right now. I was still deciding if his behavior had been enough of a red flag to break up with him and risk being single…again. I figured he wasn't going to call after the whole argument the other night, but he did. He seemed ready to move on like nothing ever happened. I was still angry with him, but I was also worried about the sudden show of jealousy. It might be best to just leave him alone…but I shuddered at the thought of going back into the dating pool. So much wasted time. And there was no guarantee I'd ever find someone else. I could grow old and end up being a cat lady…well, probably not since I don't' really like cats. Maybe I'd end up a dog version of a cat lady…

"Of course I've been missing you," he said cheerfully. He began telling me about some new project he was bidding on at work… and then I woke up the next morning, phone in hand. I wonder how long he tried to talk to me before realizing I was asleep…oh well.

I was really torn about how to handle this whole thing. On the one hand, he'd been a total ass and I really didn't like jealousy as a character trait…but on the other hand, didn't everyone act out of character on occasion? Should one misunderstanding be the end of a relationship? Maybe I could have handled the whole situation differently. Once I get mad, I get sarcastic and that never helps the situation.

"These just came in for you, Destiny," What's-Her-Face, the new temp, called out as she leaned into my office. I'd corrected her yesterday and the day before countless times. For some reason, she just couldn't remember Desiree. Then again, I had no clue what her name was, so I guess she was doing better than I was in that respect. She was holding a beautiful bouquet of flowers in a turquoise vase. It had all of my favorites. Calla lilies, dahlias, roses, and freesia. It was a gorgeous and fragrant bouquet.

"Who are those from?" Paulette called from the other side of the office, which consisted of four cubicles.

I pulled the card out and read it aloud: "Roses are red. Violets are blue. Sorry I was an asshole. You're too good to be true." Jarod's name was scrawled at the bottom. I laughed out loud at the poem and then returned to my typing.

"Wow. That's a beautiful bouquet! Not from the grocery store, that's for sure. What happened? What's he apologizing for? Are you gonna forgive him?" Paulette was known for her rapid-fire questioning, which neither I nor my office mates bothered to answer too often. She was also the office gossip. Anything you told her would be around the courthouse and in the paper by the next morning.

I hadn't really spoken to Jarod much, other than a few brief calls. He texted and asked me out several times, but I turned him down. He called a few times to chat, but I really didn't have much to say to him. I wasn't sure of what to say to him. I guess I still had a bad taste in my mouth about the other night. Who wants to go out and end up with a repeat of the last date? That was disastrous and my feelings were still a little singed, to be quite honest.

I finally finished up typing my reports when I decided to check my email. I was surprised to see an email from Jarod. This was new. We rarely emailed each other. We were more of a text or talk type of couple.

Dearest Desiree,

I behaved like a jealous teenager instead of a man. Your man. I wake up every morning and ask myself, "What does she see in you?" Then I go out and try to be a better man. Someone deserving of your beauty and passion. You are a rare, caring, and beautiful gem and I don't deserve you. I'm completely and totally in love with you, and the thought of losing you makes me crazy, which is exactly how I behaved when I saw a good-looking guy talking to you. I kept thinking, "What if she wants him instead of me?" Then I thought about how he was better looking than me. I let my imagination get the best of me and I applied a lot of characteristics to you unfairly. You've never given me any reason to doubt you. I also see you're not going to let this just blow over like I hoped. I should have known you were too stubborn for me to get back into your good graces without a grand, sweeping gesture. I hope this doesn't make you angrier, but you really are sexy when you're mad.

Anyway, this is my gesture: I've hired a chauffeur to pick you up after work today around seven. I called the house and spoke with Maia. She tells me she's going with her dad tonight, so you can't use her as an excuse :) Wear that sexy blue dress you've never taken the tags off of. We're going to dinner at Roy's and then dancing wherever you want.

I fully understand how my actions insulted you as a woman of honor, and a lady. I challenged your integrity. I forgot that I'm not dealing with just anyone off of the street. You're a true lady, which is part of what attracted me to you in the first place. I should have known better and I've been kicking myself ever since. I've never been big on apologies, I'm a proud man. I knew I owed you one, a big one, but I was just hoping you'd forgive me and move on without me having to swallow my pride and admit to sticking these size thirteens down my throat. I'm not one to beg, but please, please, PLEASE allow me the opportunity to show you that I'm a grown man. Your man. The man of your dreams. The man who will fight for you, not against you. The man who

will love your child as his own. The man who will cherish
you like the queen you are. Not a childish idiot that managed
to fuck up an opportunity with the most beautiful, sensual,
caring, kind goddess I've ever met. If I can't make things
right with you, I feel like I'll regret it for the rest of my life.
Please afford me the opportunity to make it up to you.

Love,
Jarod

Wow...I've had a few apologies in my life, but this one certainly kicked the other ones' asses. I read the email about three more times. Goddess...I certainly like the sound of that. I'm a Leo, so flattery is always good for my soul. It certainly seemed like he understood why I was upset. Why would he possibly feel like he wasn't good enough for me? Who was I? I didn't have any great status or wealth or...anything. I was a single mom living paycheck to paycheck. Maybe I'd talk to him about that later. If I decided to talk to him later. Everyone makes mistakes. Wasn't he entitled to a little forgiveness? I'd give him one more chance, I decided, but if I saw any further indications he was a jealous idiot, I'd break up with him. I hit the reply button:

Jarod,
I'll see you tonight.

Desiree

I didn't want to seem too enthusiastic. Let him squirm a little. He deserved it, after all. I smiled as I closed my laptop and got ready to head out into the field for an interview.

The call seemed like a spite call to me. Someone had called in saying that his eight-year-old daughter was often left home alone and was sweeping unknown white substances off of the floor and he wanted to make sure it wasn't drugs. Couldn't you just ask her mother? It could be flour or sugar or who knows what type of harmless legal substance. But, since the call was made, it had to be investigated. And then a report had to be typed. I sighed.

So much of my work consisted of ruling out vindictive divorcees. Why can't adults just be adults when they break up (my ex and I included)? I didn't feel like it was me. I certainly wasn't the one filing all the bogus court motions, calling Child Protective Services or the police. I didn't have my mother call his mother with ridiculous claims or to tell on me if I didn't agree with him like he had done to me. My mother never liked him in the first place, she certainly wasn't going to help, but that didn't stop him from trying. I never understood why he found it necessary to go through all of that. The whole process was ridiculous and I just wanted to be done with him. If I didn't believe in karma and I knew a hitman... well, maybe I wouldn't go as far as a hitman, but it certainly brought a smile to my mood. I mean, I'd never physically hurt him, but sometimes the visualization of a plan was a great source of amusement. Once, I'd gone as far as to create him as a character on my computer game, The Sims, turn him into a vampire, and then let him die in the sun. But that was about as much hostility as I could muster. As much as I couldn't stand Maurice, he was Maia's father. And he was the only one she'd ever have. I sighed and wished I could go shake the shit out of myself fourteen years ago when I met him. Maybe I could invent a time machine...nah. Then I wouldn't have Maia, and she was worth whatever penance I had to pay. Well, that and I'd failed all my college science classes and I had no idea how to build anything. I didn't want to imagine my life without her anyway. She was the definition of a silver lining. I never for one second regretted Maia, and so no matter how much I wished I never met Maurice, it meant life without Maia. And that was just not a reality I ever wanted, no point in even daydreaming about it.

I closed the door on that line of thought and headed out to go check out the case of the suspicious white powder.

*   *   *   *   *

Ann Rivera was one of the most unusual people I'd ever interviewed. She was a pediatric nurse, but also an "intuitive tarot reader" in her spare time. I know what tarot cards are, but I have no idea what the difference between a regular tarot reader and an intuitive tarot reader is. When I asked her about the white powder, she laughed before answering me. She was not your typical interviewee. They're usually not friendly or personable and all too often seem like they have the weight of the world on their shoulders. Ann was practically glowing with a calm sort of happiness. She explained with a chuckle that about once a month, she sprinkles her floors with a homemade blend of Epsom salt, baking soda and essential oils. She lets it sit for a few minutes, and then sweeps it up. "It takes all of the stuck energy and negativity with it," she said. "I package it and sell it at the New Age store over on Monument. You should go by there sometime. The owner is great. It's called Rafaela's Hands, if you ever want to check it out." I smiled at her. No point in telling her I was close friends with the owner and I knew both the shop and the floor sweep well. The house smelled amazing. I was definitely going to get some of that floor sweep the next time I went by the shop. Between damp swimsuits and my dog Penzy, my house could use a little freshening. I proceeded with the interview and concluded that Ann's daughter, Shelly, had never been left home alone. Her father lived 45 minutes away, rarely saw her, and in fact hardly even called her. He took Ann to court recently trying to get a reduction in child support, not realizing Ann knew about a second job he held. Since he had opened the door for a modification, the amount of child support he was paying was actually raised since he wasn't upholding his part of the visitation deal and had significantly increased his income. Obviously, he wasn't happy about it. The two had argued and he vowed he'd get even with her.

"He never was the best at dealing with his anger. He'd lash out and act without thinking. It was a major part of the reason we got divorced. Once he started lashing out at me, I filed for divorce and never looked back," she explained. "I used to get really upset by all of the false accusations, court dates, and drama. Then I realized that the less I let his negativity affect me, the less he bothered. He still flares up from time to time, but at this point, it really doesn't upset me. I answer whatever questions are asked, complete whatever interviews, take whatever drug test, and then continue about my business. I always see him coming and he never wins. He'll leave me alone soon. He's learning."

She sounded so certain about that statement. I wished I could have sounded so certain when I went through all the drama with Maurice. I stressed out until I lost patches of hair and had to be put on anti-anxiety medication. Something about Ann's demeanor was just so different from what I usually encountered. She was positively serene, as if she'd figured out all the secrets in life and was watching everyone else try to figure it out. Whatever she knew, I needed to figure it out.

I fingered the business card she'd given me as I was leaving. She'd handed it to me and said, "When the time comes, and you'll know when it has, know that you are brave enough, strong enough, and smart enough." I was so astounded, I just stood there on the front porch with my mouth agape. "When the time comes, you'll know exactly what I'm talking about. Goodbye, Ms. Kane. I hope we meet again under more pleasant circumstances. You take care of yourself." And then she softly closed the door, leaving me to stare at the colorful stained-glass inserts on the beautiful oak door.

What was she talking about? Was this something she did to get clients? Drop some piece of ambiguous advice and have them come see you for clarification? She had no way of knowing who was coming to interview her until I called earlier today to find out when would be a good time to interview her and Shelly. I was completely floored. Ordinarily, I throw cards away when I get them from interviewees. But if they were relevant, then they went into the case file and stayed in my cabinet at work. But today, I found myself tucking this card into my wallet. I mused about it the whole way home.

CHAPTER 6

After work, I decided I needed some advice about what to wear and what to say to Jarod during this reunion, if that's what it ended up being. I took Penzy out for her walk and then gathered a few outfit options and my make-up bag and headed back for the car. I needed reinforcements. Jarod texted me that the car would arrive around 7:30, which left me a little over two hours. I decided to call one of my best friends, Luna, to help me decide.

I always loved going over to Luna's house, which was about 15 minutes from my place, but I didn't want to have the car waiting for me. Luna lived with her husband, Pete, and their eight-year-old daughter, Celeste, in a big old house in Northwest Baltimore.

You know how old houses kind of get that…old house smell? Well, hers didn't have it. I asked her about it once, and found out you could freshen up the house by adding essential oil to baking soda and Epsom salt and simply scattering it across the floor, and then sweeping the floor. Then she explained further, "I find that making all of my own cleaning products has become quite a magical experience." She laughed at her own private little joke before she continued. Luna made cleaning her house into some sort of ritual she truly enjoyed. Every scent had a purpose. Everything was put in a place intentionally. Luna had studied *feng shui* and had applied it throughout her entire house. Her house was like a fantasy land.

Beautiful, healthy houseplants in all of the windows. She had them hanging from the ceilings in sunny areas. Every single window had some kind of greenery flourishing in front of it. She had stands, urns, and beautiful ceramic pots, each one with some lush, exotic looking plant thriving in it. She and Anna Rivera would probably have gotten along fabulously.

All three of my houseplants were in plastic pots. They were on countertops and the floor of my kitchen. My landscaping was great. Houseplants...not so much. Looking at her exotic assortments of plants and containers, even though my plants were healthy, I almost felt ashamed of mine. The house was big, but somehow cozy at the same time. She had crystal clusters, salt lamps and incense bowls in just about every room of the house. And each room somehow had its own inviting, spicy scent. No one room smelled the same as the other.

"I can't believe he sent flowers to your job!" Nika exclaimed. "That's so romantic!" Nika, Luna and I had been friends since college. Luna Montgomery (she was Sharron Johnson when we met, but after undergoing some spiritual development, she changed her name to Luna, and after marrying she changed the last name to Montgomery), Nika and I had all lived together our junior and senior years of college. We had a suite, a nicely sized room with a little sitting area and two small bedrooms with our bunk beds in them. With the tiny kitchenette and miniscule bathroom, it almost could have been mistaken for a small apartment. There were four of us in the suite.

We really lucked out in getting the room our junior year because the suites were usually reserved for seniors. It was a happy accident. There was some sort of clerical error that lead to several students not having rooms the day we were supposed to move in. So there we all stood, in the campus housing office, nervous and angry. We were randomly assigned to spare dorms. A few students even had to stay in local hotels until the whole mess could be sorted out. A group of about twenty juniors ended up getting rooms in the suites that semester, and I was one of the lucky ones. Luna was my roommate. Nika was rooming with Amelia West. The two of them didn't get along well at all…actually, none of us got along with her. Amelia was gorgeous, and she knew it. She was the head cheerleader, a sorority girl, and very popular. She always had a constant swarm of people around her. Several members of the football team, most of the cheerleaders, and loads of sorority girls were constantly in the suite.

When we'd first approached her about the amount of time she had guests, how much time she spent on the phone, the state she and her numerous guests left the kitchen in, and how long she'd hog the bathroom, she looked at us as if we had insulted her by speaking to her. As if she thought we weren't of a high enough caliber to speak to her.

Luna and I were more laid back and would go back into our room to try to figure out what else to say, another way to get our point across peacefully. Nika, on the other hand, was not about to be snubbed by anybody. Nika had grown up in the projects in New York City and was no stranger to a tussle. In fact, she seemed to welcome the occasional fight just to make sure she still had it. Luna and I invited Nika to join us in an intervention with Amelia. "Fuck that," Nika said, "Imma let that bitch know she got two choices. Either she gets her shit together and starts treating this place with some respect or Imma beat her ass and teach her some respect. Real talk." Luna and I pleaded with her to keep things non-violent. "You could end up expelled or arrested!" Luna gasped in her sweet voice. She always sounded like a little girl, or maybe a fairy or something. She always sounded sweet, like she had a little piece of sunshine she was ready to share with everyone. "Or even worse!" she continued, "You could be expelled *and* arrested."

Luckily for us, a few days later, Amelia was suspended for some prank she had the new pledges participate in. We sat together eating snacks, laughing, and joking as we watched Amelia while she packed and sobbed alone. No one lifted a finger to so much as open a door for her. Somehow, that experience had bonded us together for life. We even got an apartment together after graduation.

"This is so exciting! Nothing like that ever happens to me anymore," Nika pouted for a brief second and then took a sip of wine. Tanika Alexander was Tanika Nichols when we all took a trip to Atlanta. We had a blast. Rooftop pools, lounges, concerts, massages, restaurants...and of course lots and lots of vodka. We went to some ultra-exclusive lounge that she heard of from a friend of a friend, who just happened to know the bouncer. Anyway, she hit it off with the bartender, who turned out to be the owner and now she is married and lives in Atlanta. Jesse was an alright guy. Better than alright. He treated her well and was a responsible husband and father. He was just...unimaginative. Nika still lived vicariously through me as I struggled my way through the jungle that is dating. Nika, Luna and I Facetimed at least once a month, and talked all the time, but I still missed having my best friend around.

"Should I wear the dress?" I bought the royal blue dress when we went on a quick trip not too long after I got separated. At the time, she was single and I was too for the first time in a decade. I left Maia with my parents in Connecticut and we went to Atlanta and had a blast. We went shopping and, while feeling that vacation boldness, I bought a dress I never would have worn before. It was shorter than I generally wore, about wrist length, but it was also backless and hugged my curves like a nervous preschooler. I couldn't believe how sexy I looked in it in the dressing room, so despite the $220 price tag, I bought it. When I got home, every time I put it on, I felt like a fraud. Desiree Kane plays the role of sexy woman…unconvincingly. I've just never felt like I could fully pull it off, so although I try it on from time to time, I'd never worn it out.

"Yes!" Nika shrilly exclaimed. "Desi, you've had that thing for like, two years! It's time to wear it out. You look fantastic in it! I wish I still had a shape for it. Why didn't you tell me having a baby would make me so fat? I know! Wear it with those strappy gold sandals, the really sexy high ones we got on sale at the outlet that time. Oooh! Do you have a flower or barrette or something? You should pull one side of your fro back! You're going to look so amazing! This is going to be so much fun! A chauffeur! This guy sounds like a keeper." I'm pretty sure she was more excited than I was. Nika was a consultant for a company that sold products for couples…or that you could use alone, if you wanted to. She was doing really well and was able to quit her full-time job as a paralegal and stay home with her 18-month-old son, Justin.

"I just don't know if I can pull it off," I said skeptically. I felt like I was playing dress up for a role I wasn't mature enough for yet. I've never been the sexy dress type.

"You've been saying that same crap since college!" Nika leaned forward to make sure I could tell from the screen that she was rolling her eyes.

"You really have," Luna chimed in with her whimsical laugh.

"Shoot! Justin's up," Nika said quickly. "I gotta go. Take a picture and send it to my phone. Your ass had better have that blue dress on when you step out of that door! You aren't playing sexy. You *ARE* sexy. Own it! Have fun. Do everything I would do! Love you! Bye!" Nika had always been a fast talker and a fiercely loyal friend.

"Fine! I'll wear it," I laughed. "Love you, too!" I turned my tablet off and then went to get dressed. I figured, if I was playing the part of sexy, I'd do it right. I started with a quick shower and moisturizing, because ash is never sexy. I put on a lacy g-string and some perfume, which I rarely bothered to wear. I carefully applied make up and got dressed, including the gold strappy heels. When I was finished, I looked at myself in the full-length mirror. I almost didn't look like I was pretending to be sexy, I thought. I checked the time. I had about ten minutes to spare. I snapped a few selfies and sent them to Nika before checking my purse to make sure I was ready for the evening. I debated on whether or not I should wear a sweater. The dress was amazing and bold. I couldn't cover it up. Maybe I'd wear a shawl. Was that getting too dressy?

"What do you think? Too much?" I asked my beagle, Penzy, after I put on the shawl. She responded by staring for a second and then walking over to her bed in the corner and curling up for a nap. Clearly, she'd be no help. Maybe I just needed to wear something else...

"Don't even think about changing out of that dress!" Luna scolded as if she could read my mind. "You look amazing," she said with a smile.

Just then, the doorbell rang letting me know it was definitely too late to punk out of wearing the dress. I took a deep breath and opened the door.

Jarod was standing there wearing a dark suit with a tie, looking good enough to take a bite. "Damn, baby, I knew you'd look good in that dress, but I didn't know you'd look *this* good. If I didn't have all this making up to do, I'd try to take you inside and see what you have on under that dress." Oh, he'd definitely like what I had on under the dress...nothing but a lacy, black g-string. "Thank you, you don't look too bad yourself," I replied with a smile.

"Oh, hey Luna," Jarod waved to her with a smile as she grabbed her purse to head out the door.

"Hey Jarod. You clean up nicely," she said with a smile. "Well, you two have fun. I have to go pick Celeste up from ballet. Penzy can come home with me for the night, just in case."

She gave me a peck on the cheek and a smile that said I'd better have fun, waved at Jarod, and then she and Penzy walked to her car and drove off.

Jarod took my hand and escorted me to the black Towncar waiting at the end the small driveway I had put in when I realized what parking in this neighborhood often looked like. I hadn't had this much fanfare since my wedding. Clearly, that hadn't worked out, so I decided not to draw any more parallels between the two events. He really had gone all out. Jarod hated wearing ties. The only time he ever wore them was when he had to meet with stakeholders on the projects he was working on. He really was going out of his way to make a good impression. Hopefully I had made a better choice this time than the many times I'd forgiven Maurice for one hurtful act after another. I prayed I was making the right choice by giving Jarod a second chance. I just didn't want to end up hurt and having to start all over again. The thought of ending up alone in life made the hole deeper. It made the bottom seem that much further down.

*　*　*　*　*

We had a fantastic night. After dinner, drinks, and an amazing chocolate lava cake that was to die for at Roy's, we went dancing. And had more drinks. We went back to his place since we were both pretty tipsy and he lived closer than I did to the nightclub. By the time we got back to his house I was ready to kick off my shoes and put my feet up. I went for the couch immediately to do exactly that. He instantly lit a few candles around the room and poured me another vodka and cranberry. Without saying a word, he pulled my feet into his lap and began giving them a massage. Sweet baby Jesus, did that feel amazing!

"Mmmmm. That feels great. Thank you." I leaned my head back against the cushions of the plush sectional sofa and closed my eyes. The relaxation and soft, sensual contact, along with the vodka, had me suddenly not-at-all tired as he rubbed my feet. I found myself daydreaming about him working his way up my leg with the firm, arousing pressure. Like a mind-reader, his fingers began to work their way up to my ankles, then my calves. I began to squirm in my seat as his slow, steady pressure began to work its way further up my leg.

"I really did miss you," he began. "You were so mad at me, I wasn't sure you'd give me a second chance."

"I wasn't sure I was going to either," I answered honestly with a laugh. Nika got on me about my honesty all the time. I was pretty much an open book in a relationship. "You tell him too much! And why is he even asking about details from your past relationships?" she asked. He knew about my past few relationships and how they ended. I didn't see the big deal. I knew about his, too.

"Well, I'm glad you did. I know we haven't been together too long, but the thought of losing you is...intolerable to me," he said as he continued to massage my feet. "I got home and started kicking myself for being such an idiot. You're the perfect woman. I decided I had to do whatever I had to do to get you back. I'm in love with you." He stopped massaging and looked into my eyes. I wasn't sure how to respond. I mean, sure I really liked him, and cared a great deal for him. But was I in love with him? I was definitely getting there before this big argument. Was he expecting me to say it back? My head was swimming with champagne from dinner and vodka from the rest of the evening. Surely I couldn't be expected to make a clear decision on the spot, not now.

He saved me the trouble of thinking by saying to me, "I'm not done apologizing yet. You want this on the couch, or upstairs?" as he leaned with his head between my thighs and reached up my dress, slowly tugging my panties down.

CHAPTER 7

"Wake up! Desi, wake up! Come one! We gotta get out of here!"

Someone was fiercely shaking my shoulder. Tearing me away from a fantastic, heavy, dreamless sleep. The combination of good sex, vodka, and exhaustion had me slow and heavy.

"What? What is it?" I slurred thickly, willing myself to the surface from my sleep. I rolled over, peeking one eye open. Jarod was leaned over me shaking me with one hand and pulling the covers off with the other.

"Fire! We gotta go!" he said.

Fire? I bolted upright, fully alert now. I could smell smoke. I looked at the bedroom door and saw curls of smoke creeping in under the doorway. Oh my God! Were we trapped?

"Here," he said, throwing my dress at me. I quickly pulled it over my head and got up.

"Can we go that way? There's smoke coming in from the door," I said, struggling to think rationally. I swallowed the panic I felt rising up my throat.

"I don't know," he said, heading to the door. He touched the knob, but quickly pulled his hand away. "It's hot."

Smoke was pouring in now. I grabbed the comforter off of the bed and stuffed it into the space between the door. That would at least slow the smoke from coming in. How were we going to get out? Think Desi, think!

"Did you call 911?" I asked. Maybe they'd get here before we died of smoke inhalation. The comforter had slowed it down, but it was still getting smoky in the room.

"Yes. They're on the way, but who knows when they'll get here." He paced back and forth for a few seconds. "Baby, I love you. I'll get you out of this. This is not what I had planned."

I thought of Maia. No was way I going to leave her. I had to figure this out. I looked at the back window.

"We can go out this window!" Jarod said following my gaze. We headed to the window in the back of his bedroom. We were on the second story above a small patio and then sloping hill in the back yard. Oh, shit. I was gonna break my legs, but it was better than burning to death.

He opened the window and pushed out the screen. "I'll lower you as far as I can, then I'll jump."

He ran back into the room and began pushing the bed towards the window. "I'll use this to brace my feet so I don't fall out of the window." He looked deep into my eyes for a minute and wiped the tears that I didn't realize were streaming down my face. "Trust me, okay?"

"Okay," I whispered. It was a better plan than waiting to see if we died of smoke inhalation before the fire department arrived. Did I trust him with my life? I guess I had no choice.

He folded a blanket over the window-sill. "Back out slowly and I'll lower you." He grabbed my wrists and I grabbed his. He gave me a quick reassuring smile, and then said," Okay, baby, now."

I was backing out slowly, terrified. What if he dropped me? What if I broke my back and was paralyzed? What if I died? Had I told Maia that I loved her today? I wished I'd hugged her a little longer.

I screamed a little when I backed completely off of the ledge. Holding onto his wrists as hard as I could, I dangled there with the cool night air. I looked down at my bare feet suspended a good ten feet above the ground. I used to fall off horses all the time, but this was different. Falling off of a horse was never planned. You didn't have time to be scared because you generally didn't see it coming until it was too late. Yes, this was definitely much different. This was much higher…this was fucking terrifying.

I looked back up at Jarod and saw smoke beginning to billow out of the window around him. Was the room on fire now, too? He looked so calm as he continued to lower me from the window. How was he so calm? I felt like my heart was going to explode. And how was he going to get out of there?

"That's as low as I can get you, Desi," Jarod said, his voice straining a little.

"How are you going to get out?" I asked, realizing now that this may be the last time I saw Jarod.

"Don't worry about me. I'll get out," he said. "Ready?"

Hell no I wasn't ready. I looked down and saw that I was still about eight feet above a concrete patio. Here goes nothing. I closed my eyes and said a quick prayer. I gave him a quick nod as I mentally sent my love to Maia, and then I let go…

*   *   *   *   *

"Ma'am? Ma'am? Can you hear me? Ma'am? Can you squeeze my hand, ma'am? Squeeze my hand."

I felt like I was deep under murky water, trying to swim to the surface. There were sounds and feelings, but I couldn't make them out. I tried to go back to sleep but someone was squeezing my hand. Some woman was talking to me. Where was I? I was freezing. I was cold and lying on something hard. I tried to turn my head toward the voice, but I couldn't. I seemed to be strapped down and my neck was in some sort of brace.

"Ma'am? Can you hear me? Squeeze my hand if you can hear me." Why was she yelling at me? I just wanted to go back to sleep. I squeezed a latex gloved hand, hoping it would shut up so I could go back to sleep.

"Good! We got a strong response," the voice said to someone over her shoulder. "Vitals are good."

Where was I? I felt like my eyelids had been glued shut. I struggled to open them. I was lying on the ground outside strapped to a board. Emergency workers were everywhere. My eyes began to close again, and then they flew open as my memory flooded back to me.

"Where's Jarod?" I croaked. I didn't sound anything like myself. The last thing I remembered was seeing him hanging out of the window with a blanket of smoke pouring out of the window behind him.

"He's okay, Ma'am. He's getting checked out a little ways away. He's been asking about you." She smiled at me reassuringly before going back to the clipboard she was using to record whatever she was writing.

"My head hurts." The more awake I became, the more I noticed that I hurt all over. My left ankle felt like it was being bathed in waves of white-hot fire. I'd never been more miserable in my life. I was freezing, I had a killer headache and I was nauseous.

"You had quite a fall. We're going to get you to the hospital soon, we just needed to be sure you're stable enough to move. You were really brave to jump from the window. Not sure if you'd have made it if you hadn't."

"Where am I?" I asked. I knew I had to be somewhere around Jarod's house, but I couldn't turn my head to look and figure it out.

"We're in the parking lot in front of the community. It's a pretty serious fire. We had to evacuate the whole row of townhouses."

"How did it start?" I asked. Whoa…After I'd spoken that last sentence, I felt incredibly dizzy. I was pretty sure I had a concussion. I'd had a few concussions before from falling from my horse when I was younger. It was a relentless headache that lasted for at least a week…great.

"That's under investigation, Ma'am," she said.

I couldn't think of anything else that I felt like going through the effort to ask. A male paramedic joined the lady and they began poking and prodding me, taking vitals and shining lights in my eyes as they spoke to each other. My head was killing me. I didn't care what they were saying. I just wanted to go back to sleep and wake up somewhere warm and safe. Like Tahiti. I answered all of their questions, which felt like they were asking me the same thing over and over. Every time I tried to close my eyes, one of them would start ma'am-ing me until I opened them again. They were pretty sure I had a concussion too, so I wasn't allowed to go to sleep. Fantastic. I got to stay awake to freeze to death after almost burning to death. How could I possibly be so lucky?

"Sir!" the male paramedic exclaimed. "Give us a few more minutes! I promise you, we're taking the best care of her that we possibly…" He abruptly stopped and suddenly, Jarod came into my line of view.

"Desi! Are you okay?" He leaned over me, allowing me to see a crudely taped gauze pad on his forehead.

"I don't know," was all I could say. I felt awful that I didn't want to say more, but it was just too much effort. It was getting harder and harder to stay awake, and honestly, I didn't want to. I closed my eyes and allowed the darkness to settle back over me like the warm blanket I wished I was under.

CHAPTER 8

"Can I get you anything else?" Jarod asked me for the um-teenth time. He already made Maia and me oatmeal, fresh fruit, eggs, and turkey bacon for breakfast. He even carried me downstairs to the couch in the living room so I wouldn't have to hobble. He fluffed my pillows, dropped Maia off at school after carefully lining up the newspaper, remotes, my phone, laptop and Kindle along the sectional sofa where I was stationed in front of the television. He even plugged the chargers in and draped the cords over the arm of the couch so I wouldn't be inconvenienced by low batteries. In the interest of convenience, since he had no place to stay and I had no way to get around, we decided he'd stay with me until I got back on my feet. It had been ten days since the fire. I spent a week in the hospital and was relieved to be home.

"I'm fine, really. Relax. Sit down," I chuckled. Since being released from the hospital, Jarod had attended to my every need, even ones I hadn't thought about. He went out and got Epsom salt and white vinegar for me to sponge bathe in so I wouldn't be quite so sore. He got my favorite Ben & Jerry's, my favorite potato chips, a stack of DVDs I'd been meaning to catch up on, a few books he thought I'd be interested in, plus a few I'd been meaning to read but hadn't found the time. I'd never been so spoiled in my life. If it weren't for the pain of my broken ankle, bruised ribs, and the never-ending headache, I'd have felt like I was on a stay at home vacation.

I awoke in the hospital the morning after the fire. At first, I wasn't quite sure where I was. I looked slowly around, taking in the muted pastels of the wallpaper and chairs. I saw the hospital bed I was in before realizing I was attached to an IV. There was that quiet sense of hurry always present in hospitals. That feeling that makes everything seem so much more serious and sterile. I've always hated hospitals. The smells, the feeling of sadness that hung in the air and seeped into the walls. The pain that was always around the corner. This was my first stay in the hospital since I'd had Maia. I hoped it would be a fast one.

I was told I was incredibly lucky and brave over and over again. That was how everyone described me. A parade of doctors, fire investigators, nurses, family and friends all came in one by one. All of them told me how incredibly brave I had been and how lucky I was to be alive. I had a broken ankle, sprained wrist, bruised shoulder and ribs, and a mild concussion. Every time I moved, a new rainbow of pain sprung up behind my eyes as I flinched. I felt like I'd been hit by a bus. I've learned from falling off of horses that you never know until two days later how much you're actually going to hurt. It takes that long for the soreness to set in. I'd never hurt so badly in all my life.

Most of my stay was a blur, thanks to the pain medication I was getting. Every time I awoke for long enough to account for who was around, Jarod was there. I'm not sure how he got around the visiting hours, but he never left my side. If I groaned, he wanted to know why. If I was hungry, he got me food. He had managed to quickly tie some sheets to the bedpost, which allowed him to lower himself from the window. The sheets had slipped while he was climbing down, and he had fallen, leaving him with a gash on his forehead and a sprained elbow. All things considered, he made out better than me. Then again, I had a home to return to. His entire house had been gutted by the fire, which also damaged the houses on either side of it. He said he had a hotel room nearby, but as far as I could tell, he never went to it. The only time he left my side was when my parents came in from Connecticut. They also had a nearby hotel and came and stayed during part of visiting hours. I awakened at one point to see Jarod and my parents involved in a great conversation. They were laughing and talking like they'd known each other for years. When I was released, he assured them he wasn't leaving my side. They all exchanged numbers and emails, and they went back up to Connecticut.

Maia, Maurice, and I went to see them fairly often before the divorce. They purchased an adorable three-bedroom split-level cottage overlooking a small lake in northwestern Connecticut. Maia loved the quaint little town. I had to admit, it was a definite vacation from Baltimore. In the winter when the chimney was lit and smoke curled towards the grey sky, it looked like a Thomas Kinkade painting. It felt like watching a movie set in some perfect little town with old Victorian houses and colorful storefront shops. I enjoyed it for about a week at a time, but then I was ready to get back to a little hustle and bustle. Mom and Dad felt quite the opposite, and rarely traveled out of the area anymore. This was quite the occasion for them to have been in town, but unfortunately, I slept through most of their visit. I was glad they got to spend some time with Maia before they had to go. They'd have stayed longer, but Mom had to get back for mid-terms. She had decided to spend her retirement teaching English at the local community college. She said it let her feel almost retired, but not too retired. Dad spent his time fishing, reading, working on old cars, and doing whatever else he felt like doing. He wanted to feel all the way retired. I was smothered in lots of hugs, kisses, and advice before they headed back to the airport.

I spent most of my time sleeping the first day home from the hospital. I planned to follow suit for the next day too. I pretty much napped until it was time to take more painkillers or unless Jarod made me wake up to eat or go to the bathroom. He tried to keep me company on the couch for a little while, but I really couldn't keep my eyes open. If I tried to let the painkillers wear off so I could keep him company, I started to understand just how hurt I really was. I only tried letting the medications wear off once. After that, I was lousy company because I took them on time every time. The doctors advised I should take the pills every four to six hours for at least the first three days. I'd stick to that.

CHAPTER 9

"Mom, are you sure you're ready to go back to work?" Maia asked me as we stood in my small walk-in closet trying to figure out what I could wear with my knee-high cast and sling on my arm. "You can't even stand all the way up. And it hurts you when you move! I think you should listen to Jarod. You need to stay home." It was true, I was still sore…more than just sore. I was in pain, but I was also out of leave. It was time to get back to work, and how I felt didn't really matter at this point. Time to put on the big girl panties and suck it up.

Jarod had been staying with me for a month now. More than once, he'd brought up making this living situation permanent. We were getting along great, he could help ease my financial burden, and he was into all of that manly stuff (like killing spiders, mowing grass, taking care of cars, taking out the garbage). He had some valid points, especially with the spiders. I hate spiders.

I cared for him a lot, truth be told. I was even pretty sure I had fallen in love with him. I enjoyed spending time with him, but I wasn't sure I was ready for him to move in. After all, what kind of message was that sending to Maia? Then again, was it really any different than his having stayed with us for a month? We were sleeping in the same room and all of his belongings, not that he had much left, were put away comfortably with my things. Still, we hadn't even been together a year. I really did like him…maybe

I even loved him. But was that really enough to move him in with me?

I turned on my crutches and hobbled over to the edge of my bed. I patted a spot beside me and Maia joined me. "I'll be fine," I told her, even though I wasn't really sure that statement was true. "I'm just going to do office work until I can get around better. I can't go out into the field like this."

She looked at me with a look she must have learned straight from my mother and said, "You shouldn't be going anywhere like this."

"I don't really have a lot of choice in the matter. I have bills that have to get paid. I can't get paid to stay home any longer. I have to go back to work. It doesn't make me happy, but that's really all there is to it." I hated that my child was worrying about me like she was the parent. I really hated that I was about to go back to work. I thought about the long walk down the hall to get to my office. The only thought worse than that was the long walk from the parking lot to get to the long hall. I mentally kicked myself for getting rid of the accident insurance I used to keep. It was a decision made when I was ending up with negative account balances every month. I had to trim the fat, and at the time, it had seemed like fat. I sure wished I could have that Aflac duck screaming at me now.

It certainly would ease my financial burdens if Jarod moved in. But there was so much more to that decision than just a financial standpoint. I had three bedrooms, one of which was set up as an office and exercise room. If Jarod moved in, where would his son stay when he came to visit? His nine-year-old son, Khalif, lived in San Antonio with his mother. He spent the summers with Jarod. Where would he stay? What if he didn't like me? What if his mother didn't like the idea of him staying here for the summer? We hadn't even met, after all. Then there were the what ifs...What if he moved in and Maia got really attached to him and then it didn't work out? What would my parents think? They hadn't raised me to be the type to "shack up." Was I really ready to deal with everyone's judgments?

"You're a grown ass woman! Who cares?" Jarod said when I mentioned my parents. I cared! I could just hear my mother now, lecturing me on how I was raised better. Then my father would call to fuss at me for upsetting my mother…and then she'd call my pastor. Oh, Lord. Even though I rarely went to church anymore because of swim meets, work emergencies, and a general lack of sleep, from time to time my mother would be worried enough to call old Pastor Stevens and then he'd call me. We'd gone to the church since I was twelve and despite my age, I think Pastor Stevens still thought of me as Little Desi Greene. My parents did, too. They tried to talk me out of marrying Maurice, but I was just so in love. Or so I thought. Really, nothing tragic had happened to end the relationship, so it just continued. Eventually, it seemed like marriage was the next logical step. Living with someone was pretty close to marriage in my book. Was I ready to marry Jarod? Definitely not yet. But, he'd been living here for a month now, and frankly, I liked having him there. He was considerate and thoughtful and fun to be with. I hadn't seen any signs of jealousy, so I guess it really was just a bad night.

After dinner that evening, Jarod brought it up again. "Desi, it's crazy for you to even think of going to work in your condition! You're still in pain. You can't be driving around to walk around and inspect people's lives! You're not even supposed to be driving." He scratched the back of his head, a gesture I noticed he made frequently when he was upset about something. "What kind of man would I be if I allowed my lady to put herself through that?"

"The kind who has his own life to rebuild and his own problems. You don't need to take me on as some kind of charity case. I'm not going to have you move in just because I'm out of leave. That's a horrible reason to commit to moving in with someone!" I hated borrowing money from people. I'd rather be in debt than take money from my parents, or in this case, Jarod. I had to borrow money from my parents during the divorce. I couldn't afford our house alone and the legal fees were crushing. I had a tidy little savings account, but these days, I was lucky if I had $300 in it. I realize it's a lot more than many people have, but it certainly wasn't a secure feeling. It didn't take much to wipe out $300. I had it happen time and time again. Every time I saved a little, the car would need service or Maia had some swim meet out of state and we had to pay for the bus and lodging. It was something I'd almost come to expect. As soon as soon as I was just about comfortable, something would happen and knock me straight on my ass.

"Baby, I'm not trying to pressure you into anything. And you're no charity case. You're my lady, my boo. You're strong and smart and independent and I love you for it. But just look at you. You're in no condition to go back to work. How are you going to get to your calls? Let me help you. I haven't found a new place anyway. Let me help you," he pleaded with me.

"How can you help me? You have to use that insurance money to replace your lost things. You've got to be running out of leave at work by now. How can you afford to take care of me?" I asked.

"Well, about that...I've been meaning to talk to you about my job. I wasn't totally honest with you about that," he said with a sheepish grin.

"What do you mean?" I asked, not seeing anything amusing about confessions of lying.

"Well, I don't have to worry about leave because, well, I kind of...own the company," he shrugged with a smile.

"You said you were a welder..." I began before he cut me off.

"I am. I started welding right after high school. Then I went into the military." So far, none of this was new and none of it explained how he was a business owner. And why wouldn't he have told me that?

"It's a long story I don't like to tell," he said with a sigh. "I'll tell you a short version. When I was in Afghanistan, I saved a guy's life." His eyes glazed over. His body was in the room with me, but his mind was in Afghanistan somewhere. I could tell from his eyes that what he was looking at was horrible. Maybe I didn't want to hear this story…

"We were riding in a HMMWV, that's Army talk for the armored vehicle we were in, and we drove over a landmine…" His voice trailed off. We flipped over…we were on fire…it was really bad. Some of the men were already dead when I woke up. "Charlie, that's the guy I saved…he was pinned in the wreckage. I can still smell the blood…the burning flesh…" He stopped there, lost in the wreckage on some road in Afghanistan. His facial expression didn't change, but a solitary tear rolled down his face. When it dripped off of his chin, it seemed to snap him back into reality. "Anyway," he began again, wiping his face with his sleeve "I got him out. We had to leave one of his legs behind, but I got him out. Turns out he was well off and his dad had left him a company. Not too long after we got home, he killed himself and left me his portion of the company. I've been running it with his dad ever since." I could tell from the way he abruptly ended the story that he hoped I wouldn't ask him any questions about the war.

"Why didn't you tell me this before?" I asked.

"We're a pretty successful company and do a lot of military contracting. I'm not a poor guy. It's hard for me to tell if a woman loves me for me or for my money, so I don't talk about it. That's part of why I liked you so much. You asked me what I did, but you never tried to figure out how much I made. You seemed interested in me for me, not my money. That's rare in today's day and age." He lifted my hand and pressed his lips into the center of my palm.

I was speechless. This was a lot to take in.

"Anyway, I have more than enough to take care of us all. Let me take care of you, Desi."

"Come on Mom!" Maia chimed in from the doorway. I didn't know she'd been listening in, but I was quickly discovering that eleven-year-old girls are masters of ear hustling. "You can't go back to work yet. Everything is working out great. I haven't seen you so relaxed...ever! I think you should let Jarod stay forever."

"Yeah, come on Mom!" Jarod joined in, putting an arm around Maia's shoulders. The two of them stared at me, waiting for the final verdict. This was crazy. Was I really about to extend his stay indefinitely? I had to admit, my previous reservations were definitely fading. Would my parents be upset? Probably. But I'm 35 years old. It was probably time to stop judging my actions through my parents' eyes.

"I'll think about it," I said firmly, letting them both know that the conversation was over for the evening.

Later that evening, I settled on the couch and pulled a clean sheet of paper off of one of my many legal pads and folded it in half vertically. I labeled one side "pros" and the other "cons." As I ran through the pros and cons, I couldn't find too many cons.

Pros:	Cons:
We get along great	Your family will be upset and
He is a fantastic cook	Mamma will probably tell your
Spectacular sex on demand	pastor.
Help with bills	If we break up, things will be
Help with the lawn	more difficult on Maia.
Help	If we break up, things will be
	more difficult on me.

Then across the middle, I wrote, "He's not perfect, but are you going to do better?" I stared at that question for a long time. Could

I do better? Based on what I had seen out there…based on my experience, probably not. What were my other options? I really didn't want to go back to work yet. Who was I kidding, I loved the people I worked with, but I hated my job. I had to see horrible things done to children on a regular basis. This seemed too good to be true. Well, except for the part with the broken ankle, bruised ribs and sprained shoulder.

CHAPTER 10

I awoke before Jarod did and watched him sleep for a little while. He looked so innocent, like a little boy. His bare chest rising and falling peacefully. Those well-defined abs with that little trail of hair…Well, maybe he didn't look so much like an innocent little boy. It had been six weeks since the fire and I was finally beginning to feel more myself. Everything had been perfect since Jarod moved in. He cooked almost every meal and ordered out if he didn't cook. He drove Maia to all of her practices and even dropped her off at Maurice's for me once. He did all of the grocery shopping, walked the dog, changed my oil, and mowed the lawn every week. As soon as I felt well enough to be touched… well, let's just say my nights weren't cold or lonely. Things with us certainly seemed to be solid. He seemed determined to cater to my every need. He was like a fantasy. Cooking, cleaning, helping with chores and bills, and he was sexy as hell. It all seemed too good to be true. I had come to truly appreciate and love him. I couldn't wait until I was back to moving around so I could spoil him back.

We laid up talking for hours the previous night. We spent a lot of nights up talking. Then he'd be sleepy and didn't want to get up to go to work early. "That's why it pays to be the boss," he'd say as he rolled over for a few more winks in the morning. I smiled as I thought back on the conversation from last night.

"Desi, I honestly don't know what I would have done if I'd lost you. I can't imagine my life without you and Maia. I'd just gotten you back from that stupid argument, and then I thought I'd lose you from that awful fire." He kissed my hands and then laid back into his propped position facing me. My God, did he look sexy wearing just a sheet draped over him. I mean, he had on basketball shorts, but you couldn't see that with the sheet draped over him.

"That was the scariest thing I've ever experienced," I told him honestly. "I thought I was going to die." Over the years, I'd been on my share of bucking and misbehaving horses. I'd taken some pretty awful spills and even had a concussion once. But never did I think there was the possibility of death from any of those falls. "Then when you were dropping me out of the window, I thought I might never see you again."

Even though six weeks had passed since that night, it was still vivid in my mind. Sometimes, I'd wake up in the middle of the night thinking I smelled smoke. Jarod would rub my back and tell me I was safe and to go back to sleep. Then he'd cocoon me in his strong arms and hold me against his broad chest as he went back to sleep, protecting me from my bad dreams. That was how I had begun to think of him. As my protector. I felt safe in his arms. I felt safe knowing that he was around.

"I've been thinking Desi, I mean, I know I don't really live here, but I was thinking we could get a place together. I make more than enough to support us. You wouldn't have to work. I just want to take care of you. I love you."

"Jarod, I love you too. I don't think I'm ready to quit working quite yet. I mean, what if we didn't work out? Then what would I do? I need health insurance and dental…I don't think I'm ready for that step yet," I told him honestly.

He looked almost hurt. "You don't' think we'll be together in the future?"

"Honey, we haven't been together that long. I don't see us breaking up in the future, but we haven't even been together for a whole year yet. I have a daughter to think about. And I don't want to be some kept woman. I'd have to come up with something else to do with my time and to have my own money. Even though I don't want to continue social work for the rest of my life, I like my job, and for now I need it."

"I guess you're right. You know I love Maia like she's my own daughter. I'd never let either of you want for anything. You could buy a horse and get back into riding in horse shows. I know you miss it." He presented a compelling argument... Ever since the first time I rode a horse when I was twelve, I was hooked. Somehow, no matter what else was going on in my life, I was able to tune out all of the background noise and just focus on the bond between me and my horse. I was devastated when I had to have him put to sleep almost ten years ago now. He'd broken his leg some sort of way running in a muddy field. Bubba Gump had been the best boy. Sweet and full of personality. Almost too smart to be a horse. I won countless ribbons and trophies in shows with him. I hardly ever rode anymore after putting him to sleep. I found myself comparing all others to him and it just made me sad. Only in the last few years had I begun to feel the desire to start riding again, but the funds of a single mom didn't really permit that.

"Would you feel more comfortable if we got married?" he asked. I was surprised by the thrill of joy that passed through me. My last marriage (obviously) had been a disaster. Was I really ready to think that way again? Jarod was so different from Maurice. So thoughtful and caring.

I was so glad to be out of the cast and in a slightly less intrusive orthopedic boot. It was black and covered in plastic and Velcro. If I could have jumped and clicked my heels, I would have. Very sexy...

just slightly less sexy than a hospital gown. I still had weeks of physical therapy to look forward to. Isn't that just typical of adult life. One unwanted complication after the other? I was feeling generally frumpy, useless, and unattractive. I'd been in either pajamas or sweats for weeks. Somehow, Jarod didn't seem to mind. In fact, he seemed to find the pajama and sweats look sexy. "It's easy to get you outta them pants," he laughed when I complained to him about not being able to wear any of my clothes with the cast.

I decided to take advantage of the beautiful May sun and go outside to weed my flower bed a little. I didn't realize how tired of being cooped up inside I had been until I decided to get a little air. Suddenly, I couldn't wait to feel the breeze on my face and feel the sun kiss my skin. I always loved gardening. It was like an acceptable adult version of making mud pies and playing in the dirt. I grabbed my favorite pair of cut-off shorts. They were previously my favorite pair of jeans until they had an unfortunate meeting with a bottle of bleach. I almost cried. You know when you get that one pair that always makes you look amazing, like you left trails of glitter and moonlight in your wake...this was that pair of jeans. They made cute shorts, but their former glory was definitely diminished. I grabbed a sunny yellow tank top to match the day, and one matching yellow flip flop as I prepared to go outside. "Where are you going dressed like that?" Jarod asked as I headed for the front door. He was laid back comfortably, lounged on the couch nursing a beer while he watched a basketball game. I had no idea what teams were playing and really didn't care. I'd take gardening over TV any day.

"Just going to weed my flower beds a little," I casually explained. I noticed he was still trying to do everything for me. At first it had been sweet and endearing. But now, if felt as if he was just trying to keep me inside of the house. If I wanted to go get the mail from the front porch where the mailbox was mounted near the front door, he'd do it for me.

"You don't need to be out there working. I'll do that for you." He sat his beer on a coaster on the coffee table and began to rise from the couch.

"No. I'll do it. I think I'm craving a little fresh air. I feel like I've been stuck in here forever."

"Don't you think those shorts are a little short?" he asked, like a scolding father.

I looked down at my shorts, which were about mid-thigh length. "No," I answered and put my hand on the knob preparing to go outside.

"Is there someone you're trying to show off for out there?" he asked, clearly irritated by my casual response. The way he was staring at me made me feel like I was thirteen again, arguing with my parents over the length of my skirt. I had to remind myself that I was a grown woman and could wear whatever I wanted.

I scanned my appearance again. Yellow tank top, mid-thigh length denim shorts, one flip-flop and one orthopedic boot. I didn't see anything that would be impressive to anyone. "No. If I were planning to show off, it definitely wouldn't be in this," I said with a laugh, trying to lighten the situation up a little. Maybe I was just being sensitive, but it felt like he was about to start the jealous thing again. Not since my days of high school had I had someone comment on the length of my shorts.

"So you're planning to bend over in those shorts?" he asked incredulously. Yeah...this was definitely the jealous thing again. I was finally feeling up to getting out of the house and I was not about to let his attitude stop me. I decided that I wasn't going to participate.

"Yes. Because I have no way of reaching the weeds standing up. And these aren't even short!" With that, I opened the door and began to head outside.

"Why don't you put on some jeans?" he called after me.

"Because it's 84 degrees outside, but more importantly, because I don't want to!" I turned on my good heel, hobbled off, and closed the door behind me.

*   *   *   *   *

I was just finishing up with weeding and pruning my plants in the flower bed in front of my house. It was looking neat, but just a little barren. Maybe I'd add some nice bright annuals to make the front of the house…

"Fancy meeting you here, Ms. Lady," a familiar voice said from behind, tearing me from my thoughts. I froze as still as a statue as my mind began running a hundred miles an hour. I was on my hands and knees in the dirt. Have you ever had one of those moments when the only thing you can think is "Oh shit!" Well, this was one of those moments, an OSM, as I like to call them. I wondered for a second if I was having a hallucinogenic reaction to my pain meds for my ankle. There was no reason for that voice to be near my house. How was this possible? What the hell was going on? Why was he at my house? Was he stalking me? I turned my head, and there he was, in the flesh…well so to speak. He really didn't have much more to him than bones. Byron Lee had on a pair of basketball shorts, a fresh pair of Jordans and an oversized t-shirt. Looking at his toothpick thin shins, all I could think was, "God this man is skinny." His hazel eyes twinkled in amusement as he gazed down at me.

"I knew you'd look good bent over," he said with a wide smile. "I'm gonna have to say, this is even better than I'd imagined." He licked his lips and began rubbing his palms together.

I rose to a kneeling position and stared at Byron Lee as he stood above me smiling. After what felt like an eternity, I finally found my voice. "What are you doing here, Mr. Lee?"

My mind continued to scramble, as I tried to decide if I was in any danger or not. I couldn't run with that boot on my ankle. Hell, as swollen and sore as it was, I couldn't run period.

"You know Ms. Witherspoon across the street?" he asked me, pointing diagonally across the street. "Me and her son have been friends since the 4th grade. My Mamma lives just around the corner. I saw you go in the house a few weeks ago, but I didn't want to come ring the bell." Oh, thank God. I thought he was going to say he followed me, or something. This was just a weird coincidence. At least I hoped it was. Maybe he was lying.

"Thank you for restraining yourself," I said flatly.

"You are so funny!" He threw his head back and laughed as if I'd just told a real humdinger. Then he took a step closer and in a much deeper, much more serious voice. "I bet you're a lot of fun when you decide to let your hair down, so to speak. I feel like you probably don't have fun too often. You should let me show you how to let loose." His hazel eyes twinkled seductively.

If he weighed about forty pounds more, didn't have the tattoos all over his face, and wasn't so creepy in general, his stare might have been sexy. But it wasn't. The bottom line was that his attention was making me uncomfortable. I didn't want to turn around again, because I knew he'd just have more remarks about my ass.

"Well, I just wanted to come check on you. I heard about the fire on the news. That shit was crazy! Ms. Witherspoon told me you had to jump out of a window. You're really badass." He smiled again. "I don't know no other chicks that woulda jumped out of a window." I guess that was a compliment. He sounded genuinely impressed with my badassery.

"Thank you. It was either that or burn to death, so…" my voice trailed off since I couldn't figure out how to end that sentence. In actuality, what I wanted was to end this entire interaction. "Well, I've got some things to take care of," I said to cut this awkward encounter short before it got any awkward-er.

"Do you want me to help you up?" he asked extending his hand. As much as I could have used the help, I didn't see anything good coming out of me making physical contact with him. I remembered the kiss he tried to plant on my hand the first time we met.

"I've got it, thanks," I said and struggled my way up, trying to make it appear as if it weren't a monumental task. My ribs were still a little sore and I still had a few other aches and pains. The movement of getting dressed, coming outside, and working in the garden had definitely proven to me that I wasn't as healed as I thought I was. Maybe today wasn't such a good day for gardening after all. I hobbled my way to the steps of my rowhouse and clambered up with as much dignity as I could muster. It wasn't much. I'm sure I looked ridiculous as I tried to pretend that I couldn't feel his eyes roving my back side as I walked through the door and turned to close it behind me.

"I knew you'd have pretty feet," He said with a smile. Yep. He'd just found a way to make this encounter even creepier. "I hope you can wear heels again when that ankle heals. You sho' can walk in them heels."

"Thanks. Well, goodbye," I said and closed the door.

CHAPTER 11

"Who the fuck was that?" Jarod suddenly asked. I don't even know where he came from. It's like he materialized from the walls or something. I'd just walked in, closed the door behind me, then leaned on it as relief began flooding in, not just from how much work it had been to walk up the stairs and into the house, but to have a physical barrier between me and Byron Lee. I was in the middle of my relieved exhalation when the terse question quickly snatched my breath away and I jumped with a start.

"Jesus! Jarod, I didn't see you there. You scared the crap out of me!" Although I'm sure it looked really dramatic, I instinctively clutched my hand to my heart. All I needed to do was to tell Elizabeth I was coming home because this was "the big one." I stood there for a second looking like Fred Sanford before I registered what he was saying.

After I got over the start, I took note of his demeanor. He was scowling so hard, he looked like a gargoyle glaring at me from the edge of some old building. I could feel the heat of his anger rolling off of him in waves. His handsome face had contorted into someone I didn't even recognize. He was…ugly…menacing… scary. When he spoke again, his lips were pulled back from his clenched teeth. "I said," he began slowly, taking a step toward me, "who the fuck was that?"

"Someone I know from work," I answered. The details of my calls were strictly confidential. I certainly wasn't supposed to identify anyone.

"Doesn't look like someone you'd work with to me. You think I'm stupid?" Although it hadn't seemed possible, his scowl deepened.

"He doesn't work in the office. I had to interview him." I planned to leave the explanation at that. After all, it was more than I was supposed to have told him.

"So that's who you've been sneaking up in here when I'm out?" he asked. What the hell was he talking about? I spent most of my days eating, reading, napping and watching TV. My most adventurous trip was to the upstairs bathroom to take a bath with my leg hanging over the side of the tub. The effort to get in and out the tub had been herculean at first, but was just now getting to the point where it was only kind of hard and awkward.

"What are you talking about? I haven't snuck anyone over here. And why would I need to sneak anyone over here. This is my house!" The start was beginning to wear off and anger was quickly flooding in. Who did he think he was? And how dare he talk to me this way!

"You know I go walking around outside all the time. I found a used condom in the alley." He said it as if I was supposed to have a response to that. I lived in an end unit townhouse in the Park Heights community of Baltimore, if all he found was a condom, we were doing pretty well as far as I was concerned. I didn't live in the nicest neighborhood, but it wasn't like some of them. He was still looking at me waiting for a response.

"Okay...and..." I drew the words out waiting for him to finish his thought. *I know this fool is not about to ask me if I used that condom.*

But he did.

"You know anything about it?" He folded his arms like he was awaiting a confession from a busted teenager.

"Of course not, why would I? Are you serious right now?" I asked incredulously.

"I'm here all the time so maybe you didn't want the evidence in the house," he replied as if his logic actually made some type of sense.

"So I'm going to hobble down all the stairs, down to the sidewalk and hop my ass into an alley to have sex...on the side of the house...that I own...Does that honestly make any sense to you at all? Are you listening to yourself?"

"Don't try to turn this around. You seem like you couldn't get away from him fast enough. Like you didn't want to be seen with him. You were afraid I'd see him with you, huh?" His "got you" tone was pissing me off.

"I was hoping you'd come outside and rescue me from that creeper! I don't want to be anywhere near him. You saw that creepy ass man talking to me and all you did was peek through the window?" I asked.

"So if it's not him, who you fucking?" he yelled, ignoring my question.

"Last time I checked, YOU! You don't remember all the crazy angles we had to go through just to make it work with the broken ankle and all of my bruises? And you actually think that I hopped my lame ass to an alley to fuck someone on the side of my own house! You're insane!" My voice had gotten loud and shrill. Yeah, I was fully invested in this argument now.

"Come on Desi, don't treat me like I'm stupid. You've been fucking someone when I go to work. Who is he?" He glared into my eyes as if he was trying to peek into my soul.

"I don't know what you're talking about. Nobody but Luna has been here!" Why was I even trying to justify myself to him?

I hadn't done anything wrong. I guess I should have paid more attention to the night at the movie theater. He was back on that jealous rage times a million.

"You're a lying cunt!" he said with such venom that any retort withered and died with the quick gasp that I took. I just stood there staring at him. He began pacing back and forth in the narrow hallway. "All the money I just put into you making sure your every need was taken care of. All the effort and time. Bet you didn't even notice I took your car in for service, did you?" he spat at me. I couldn't drive and hadn't been in the car since the last time he took me to the doctor's office. How was I supposed to know that and… wait a fucking minute! This motherfucker just called me a lying cunt! Oh, hell naw!

"I don't know what you're talking about and at this point, I really don't care anymore. Get the hell out of my house. We are finished. Who the fuck do you think you are talking to me like some bitch off the streets? Don't ever call me again!" I began to turn around to walk away when he grabbed my arm just above the wrist. The arm with the still sore shoulder. He yanked me toward him, forcing me to take a quick step and put too much weight on my ankle. I cried out in pain, unable to take the sudden weight on it, and collapsed at his feet.

"Where the fuck are you going?" he asked me as he crouched down to get closer to my face. His face was turned into a cruel grimace as he spoke. I guess he wanted me to be afraid of him since I was on the ground, clearly not able to walk away. My shoulder and ankle were throbbing. The blood was rushing in my ears so loudly I could barely hear.

"Have you lost your mind?" I seethed at him when I'd caught my breath. Truly, I just wanted to cry. I was in so much pain and I was so hurt and angry, but I wasn't about to show him anything but the anger. "Get the hell out of my house before I call the police!"

I began to try to get up. I guess something in my struggle shifted his anger. "Here, let me help you up," he said reaching for me.

"Don't you fucking touch me you asshole!" I screamed, snatching my good arm away. He let go of my uninjured arm easily and looked down at me. Suddenly this amused look crossed his face.

"Come on, Baby, let me help you up," he said with a smile. Like the kind of smile you give to a three-year-old throwing a tantrum.

Was he serious? It was like he had flipped a switch. Suddenly, the caring Jarod I knew was back.

"Desi," he began with a smile, "Don't be stubborn. Come on, let me help you up," and with that, he picked me up from the floor and stood me up to face him.

"I'm sorry, Baby," he said to my stunned face. I couldn't even speak. I was so confused by the sudden change. Even the air in the room felt different. There had been a dark, angry fog in the room, but it had suddenly lifted. The startlingly normal moment completely threw me off guard. I felt like a computer needing to reboot. I needed more information. How did we get here? He continued to smile into my face. Clearly, he didn't seem to feel that any further explanation was necessary.

"You're sorry?" I repeated him slowly. He was *sorry*. "You go through all of that...say all of that...call me all of that, and now you're just 'sorry'? Just like that?"

"Yeah," he seemed stunned when he said it, and took a small step backward, as if he was confused by my confusion.

Was he out of his fucking mind? How could you go through all of that, be so angry that you looked like an entirely different person, then just be fine? I was as dumbfounded. I literally couldn't think of a thing to say to respond to the sudden shift.

"Let me help you to the couch. Do you need an ice pack for your ankle or anything?" He led me from the hallway into the living room and helped me sit down. "Prop up your ankle," he said as he fluffed the pillow that had become stationed on the couch.

I was suddenly chilled and gave an involuntary shiver. The outside air had been amazing with the sun heating my skin, leaving me with that warm glow feeling that you keep for a while after you've been out in the sun.

"You cold? Here." He noticed the small shiver and immediately went to the adjacent armchair and grabbed the blanket for me. He shook the fold out and covered me with it. "I think I'm going to light the grill out back. It looks like a beautiful day to grill," he said and headed for the door at the back of the kitchen that opened to my small fenced yard. The terrace was narrow, but a fantastic escape from city life. It had been what had ultimately sold me on the end unit townhouse. The privacy fence was completely lined with garden beds. I had a small bistro with a few chairs, a charcoal grill, a little swatch of grass for Penzy, and plenty of garden space. I really missed the suburbs when I'd moved to Baltimore, but the back yard gave me a little piece of the farm life that I so loved in my teens. It was a pain to move all of the pots after the divorce. I finally found my senses and got over the shock enough to function.

"Wait a minute," I said to his back as he prepared to go light the grill. "What the hell was that?" I asked him

"What was what?" he asked sounding baffled.

"You called me a cunt! You asked me if I'd had sex in an alley. You grabbed my arm and made me fall! I say 'Get out,' and instead you light the grill? What the hell is going on?" My voice was climbing again. What kind of psycho was he?

"I said I was sorry," he said simply. Like that was supposed to make everything okay.

"You've got to be joking if you think this is just over and okay," I told him incredulously. "Surely you can't think we're okay?" I'm not sure if I was asking or telling. I guess it was a combination of both. What world did he live in that he thought he could say those things, grab me and then just say "sorry" and act like it never happened?

"Why wouldn't we be? It was just an argument. No big deal. You called me an asshole. You don't see me getting all bent out of shape over it." He was so calm that it was unsettling to me.

No. Big. Deal. I shut down and had to reboot again. "No big deal?" I echoed. What the hell is going on here?

"I asked. You answered. I feel satisfied you're telling me the truth." He paused as if that was all there was to say on the matter. Then, he smiled and said, "You want steak or chicken...What about steak *and* chicken?"

"What? No! Get out of my house!" he had to be crazy. That was the only explanation for someone who could go from so angry to perfectly fine in 3.2 seconds.

"Why Desi? It was just a fight." He still wore a patronizing smile, like I was a stubborn child throwing a tantrum. As if not for one second did he think I actually meant for him to leave.

"I'm going to call the police." Where had I left my phone?

"The police?" he laughed. "And say what? That I called you a name and then apologized? I don't think they're necessary for calling a name."

"You put your hands on me! You made me fall!" I shrieked.

"Put my hands on you?" he echoed slowly. Jarod seemed to need a reboot on that statement. "I held your wrist so you didn't walk away! You're the one who's off balance and fell. I didn't throw you down. I didn't hit you. I'd never hurt you, Desi, come on. You know I'm crazy about you. I picked you up! You're just being ridiculous right now."

I just stared at him again. I was baffled. Is that what he thought had happened? As I stared at him, he stared at me. As if I was the one being unreasonable. As if I hadn't just walked into a verbal assault.

"You are something else," he shook his head and chuckled. "I'm gonna do steak and chicken. You want potatoes or corn on the grill?" He turned and walked back into the kitchen, now planning with himself since I felt like my lips had been glued shut. "You know what? Maia should be home in an hour or so. I'll just do both. You like potatoes and she likes corn."

CHAPTER 12

"And he just went out and grilled dinner? Like nothing happened?" Luna asked as if she couldn't believe what she was hearing.

"That's what I'm telling you!" I exclaimed into the phone. I was still confused and disoriented. I felt exhausted and overwhelmed.

"That's some of the craziest shit I've ever heard," Nika said in disbelief.

"Why didn't you call the police?" Luna asked.

"Wait, is he still there?" Nika interrupted before I could get anything out. When I called Nika to tell her what had happened, she immediately added Luna in on the call.

"No. He just left to go to the store to grab some beer and a few other things. Apparently, he's planning quite the feast." I sighed and rubbed my eyes behind my glasses. "After he said it, it does sound kind of ridiculous for me to call the police. It happened so fast…maybe he didn't do it on purpose."

"Desi, I think you need to get out of there. Trust your instincts. If you felt threatened, there had to be a reason for it. I'm on my way to get you," Luna said gently.

"No, I'm fine. Really. I just need to figure this out," I said absently. I was still replaying the entire scene in my mind, over and over. Trying to gain some clarity.

"Figure what out!? That motherfucker put his hands on you! You want me to call Nook Nook?" Nika was always ready for confrontation.

Nook Nook was Nika's cousin. He was about that life. He had been in and out of jail for his entire adult life and a good portion of his juvenile life as well. The last I heard, he was living somewhere in the DC area. He probably would get along great with Byron Lee.

"I don't think he'd really hurt me. It's not like he hit me," I said.

"You can't be serious, Desi. He could have really hurt you! You're in no condition to defend yourself" Luna said.

"Look, I'm not saying he wasn't wrong or that what happened was okay. I'm just saying that I don't think the police are warranted, or needed. I'm not in danger," I said rationally.

"I don't think you're really seeing the whole picture. I don't think this is finished," Luna said. I guess she was having one of her feelings.

Oh, it was finished. I was scripting my break up with Jarod in my mind. I wasn't about to forgive his behavior earlier. This was the other shoe. A glaring red flag. The straw that broke the camel's back. I didn't need any further evidence that he had some serious jealousy issues.

"I'll be okay," I told her. I could hear a car pulling into the driveway. "I think I hear Maia coming in. I'll call you tomorrow," I told Luna and Nika as I got ready to hang up.

"Be careful," Luna warned.

"Call me if you need me. Or if you change your mind about Nook Nook," Nika said before a quick "bye."

I hobbled my way to the door. My ankle was feeling really tender.

Only it wasn't Maia. When I pulled the door open, there was a tall, dark, handsome man in a suit. "Good evening, Ma'am, I'm

Detective Walter Lembo with Baltimore City PD." He quickly flashed his credentials, just like you see on TV. "I'm looking for," he paused as he looked at his phone for notes "a Ms. Desiree Kane. Is that you?" He looked a little like Denzel Washington twenty years ago, not that the current Denzel is bad looking, but this man had to be in his early to mid forties. He had begun to gray right around his temples and sideburns, giving his close cut a distinguished look.

"Um, yes," I said. What the hell? Had the neighbors called the police? Were we loud enough that they had heard our spat? And why would a detective be here for that? Usually domestic issues involved a patrol car and uniformed officers.

"I'm not sure if Mr. Kelly told you I've come by a few times to speak with you regarding the investigation of the fire at his house this past March," he looked at me questioningly even though he hadn't really phrased it as a question.

"No. I wasn't aware that there was an investigation underway. Jarod said it was determined to be faulty wiring in his new dryer." I had a sinking feeling just then, and I wasn't sure why. Why wouldn't Jarod have shared with me that there was a detective looking for me?

"I actually came to see you in the hospital as well, but you were pretty out of it. You're looking much better. How are you feeling?" He flashed a smile so quick that if I had blinked, I would have missed it. Clearly the question was out of courtesy, not because he truly cared. This man was all about business.

"Uh, much better, thank you. I mean, I'm still sore and healing, but as you can see, I can get around now."

"That's good. Ms. Kane, may I come in? This shouldn't take too long." Detective Lembo had a direct and unwavering stare. It was like he could see into my soul with his piercing black eyes.

"Sure," I said, stepping aside so he could enter. "This way," I said after he entered. I hobbled my way to the living room. As a good host, I probably should have offered the man a drink of water or something, but my ankle was really throbbing. I hoped it wasn't reinjured. I sat down on the couch. He chose the adjacent armchair.

"Ms. Kane," he began "I'm investigating the fire as possible arson. I was wondering if I could get your take on what happened that night." He reached into a pocket and pulled out a small notebook and pen. He looked at me with the pen poised, ready to begin taking notes.

"Well, I don't think there's much for me to tell. Jarod woke me up and said he smelled smoke. As soon as I woke up, I smelled it too. There was a lot of smoke coming in at the door and the door and knob were hot, so he had to drop me out of the bedroom window. That's how I ended up with all of the injuries." I felt stupid adding that last part. I'm sure he knew that's how I'd broken my ankle. Then again, I wasn't really sure what else to say. I'd spoken to the fire investigators at the hospital in between painkiller-fueled naps. I felt like I'd told the story a million times. When I'd left the hospital, I hadn't heard from anyone else. I thought that had been the end of it.

"Let's back up a little…to before the fire," he said after quickly jotting down a few notes that had to be some sort of signature short hand. I had my own version I used in the field myself. I knew better than to try to decipher his writing. "When did you get to Mr. Kelly's house that evening?"

"Um…it was late. Well, really more like early morning. Probably around one or so." I'd had plenty to drink that evening. Between the alcohol and the fire, my memory probably wasn't the most reliable.

"What did you do when you got in?" he asked as he wrote notes furiously in the little notebook.

"We'd just gotten in from dinner and dancing. We were both pretty tired and tipsy so we went to bed not too long after we got in."

"Had Mr. Kelly been drinking as well?"

"Yes."

"Who drove you to his house that night?" he asked.

"We took an Uber. He had a car pick me up for dinner."

"Sounds mighty fancy. What was the occasion?" He looked up from his notepad and waited for me to answer.

"Um...we'd had a fight. We hadn't really been speaking to each other...well, I wasn't speaking to him. This was, I guess, our make-up date."

"And you went straight to sleep when you got in?"

Wow...Did I have to tell him that we'd had spectacular make-up sex? "Um...no...I mean, we were in the bed, but we weren't sleeping." I felt so embarrassed.

"What I mean, Ms. Kane, is were both of you in bed together? Did he maybe get up and go do some laundry or to get a drink of water or anything?" If I didn't know better, I'd think there was a slightly amused twinkle in his steady gaze.

"Oh." Now I really felt stupid and embarrassed. He didn't care if we had sex. We were two consenting adults, after all. "Um, I was pretty out of it. I don't remember him getting up, but that's not to say that he didn't at some point in time."

"Okay," Detective Lembo said simply.

Okay? That was it? My mind began to kick into high gear. Arson? So they were thinking that the fire was intentionally set. But who would do such a thing? Did Jarod have enemies that I didn't know about. I didn't really know many of his friends. We'd only met casually on a few occasions.

"Do you mind if I ask you a few questions, Detective Lembo?" I asked.

"Not at all," he said. He closed the notebook and looked me straight in the eye.

"Do you think that someone intentionally set that fire?" Might as well come right out with it. No point in sugar coating.

"That's what we're investigating, Ma'am, but yes. I do believe the blaze was intentional."

"Jarod told me it had been ruled faulty wiring from his dryer. Are you telling me that isn't true?"

"We haven't given an official ruling yet, but the fire definitely didn't start from the dryer. I've spoken to Mr. Kelly a few times, but reaching you has proven to be quite…difficult." He sounded like he was choosing his words very carefully.

"What do you mean? Don't you have my number in your files somewhere? Why didn't you just call me?" I was home almost all the time, with the exception of trips to the doctor's office.

Detective Lembo sighed. His direct gaze softened a little, as did his direct tone. "Ms. Kane, I've tried repeatedly. My number appears to be blocked. I've come by a number of times, but was told by Mr. Kelly that you weren't up to having any visitors. Frankly, I was surprised to see that you appear to be in relatively good health." He was speaking to me as if there was more he wanted to say. As if he there was more to his visit than what he was telling me.

"He never told me anything about you." My mind was racing now. What was Jarod up to? Why would he keep Detective Lembo from speaking to me? Why hadn't I received any of his calls? Not having an official cause for the fire certainly explained why he hadn't received any insurance money from the fire.

"Do you know how I was able to get you today, Ms. Kane?" Lembo asked.

"No," I said quietly.

"I parked across the street and waited. Hoping you'd come out or that he'd leave so I could get to you. You're on my way home. I've been watching off and on for a few days now."

"Why wouldn't Jarod want me to talk to you?" I mused aloud. Speaking more to myself than to the detective.

"That's a very good question," he said plainly.

"Do you think Jarod set that fire, Detective Lembo?" I asked.

"We haven't made any determinations yet. I needed to speak to you, hear your take on the events of the evening."

"And now that you have? What are you thinking? Does his story pan out?"

"I can't really say one way or the other, but let me ask you this," he began. "How often do you do laundry at 1 or 2 in the morning after a night of dancing, drinking, and…making up? Would you be likely to get up and do a few loads of laundry?"

"No," I said absently as I stared off into space. My body was in the living room, but my mind was a million miles away. What the hell was going on? Was I honestly thinking that Jarod started a fire on purpose? And why would he do that? It couldn't just be about insurance money because I don't think he'd have waited until I was there to burn the house down.

"Me either. Washing socks would probably be the last thing on my mind." I could feel him staring at me with that intense gaze, but I couldn't bring myself to look back. What had I gotten myself into?

Just then, I heard the lock click in the front door. "Mom! I'm home!" Maia called as she walked through the door into the narrow foyer. She froze when she saw Detective Lembo, but she didn't say anything.

"Well, I've taken enough of your time, Ms. Kane. Let me get out of your hair," the detective said as he stood and re-buttoned his suit jacket. "In the meantime, if you think of anything at all, please don't hesitate to call me." He handed me a business card.

"I will. I mean I won't…" I fumbled over my words.

"Thank you for your time. I'll see myself out," he said as he walked away. He paused to nod at Maia and then stepped out the front door, leaving me to stare at the door as he closed it behind him.

"Who was that, Mom?" Maia asked quizzically.

"He just had a few questions about the fire," I told her. No sense in worrying her…yet. We were definitely going to have to have a talk. If I'd had any second thoughts about breaking up with Jarod, they had all disappeared after Detective Lembo's visit.

"Oh," Maia said, instantly losing interest. She'd heard enough conversations about what had happened over the last few months. I guess the novelty had worn off. "I'm going to unpack," she said. She quickly gave me a peck on the cheek and ran up the stairs to her room.

I was still sitting on the couch staring into space, lost in my own thoughts when Jarod got back. He flashed a bright smile when he saw me, then taking note of my demeanor the smile faded and he asked, "What's wrong, baby?"

"Detective Lembo just left," I said simply. I almost added "and don't call me baby," but I was more interested in his explanation than fighting about the status of our relationship. For just a flash, he looked like a deer caught in the headlights as recognition of Lembo's name hit him. If I'd have blinked, I'd have missed the momentary panic. "What did he want?" he asked casually. I noticed he had quickly composed his face.

"How is it that he's been trying to contact me, but I haven't gotten any messages? Why didn't you tell me he'd come by before?" I asked, ignoring his question. It was clear he had been hiding things from me at best…and had burned his house down with us inside at worst. But why would he burn the house down and risk our lives? Who would do something like that?

"I didn't want him to disturb you. You were healing. I didn't want you worried about his nonsense." He said it as if it was the sensible thing to do.

"But he said he's been calling my phone as well. Why haven't I gotten any messages? Have you been going through my phone?" I asked him. I wasn't really settled down from our earlier fight and I was ready to let him have it.

He blinked at me, looking wounded and bewildered. "Of course not! Why would you even ask me such a thing?

"Because you've been lying to me," I said evenly. He just looked at me as if he were trying to figure out what I was thinking.

"Let's talk after dinner," he said. Then, before I could respond he walked to the bottom of the stairs and called up, "Hey, Maia! Dinnertime! You're gonna love what I made."

He really had outdone himself with dinner. He grilled chicken and steak that was seasoned and cooked perfectly. He baked potatoes on the grill and corn on the cob. Then he'd run out to the store and gotten a delicious garden salad. He'd even gotten a carrot cake and ice cream for dessert. He had beers for us and root beer for Maia.

The two of them chatted and laughed all through dinner, but I couldn't pull myself out of my thoughts to participate. What was going on? Was the reason he was treating us so well because he felt guilty for almost killing me in a fire? It felt crazy to think that the man I'd been living with and come to love over the last few months could be capable of doing such a thing. But he'd certainly shown another side of himself earlier today.

"What do you think, Mom?" Maia asked, anxiously awaiting my answer.

"About what" I asked.

"About what we've been talking about," she said with a laugh. Then added, "Weren't you listening at all?"

"I'm sorry, Sweetie. I was lost in my own thoughts. What did you say?" I tried to snap myself back into the conversation, but I'd been so lost in my thoughts, I truly had no idea what the two of them had been talking about.

"Jarod wants to take us on a cruise this summer! Can we go? Please? I've never been on a cruise before. Madeline went on one once and said it was the best thing ever. They had a waterslide and camp for the kids! Can we go?" she eagerly pleaded at me with her beautiful, brown eyes.

"We'll see," I said evasively with a small smile. I looked at Jarod sitting at the other end of the table. He looked as happy as could be. Why was he making plans for the summer? Didn't he hear me break up with him?

"Awe, come on, Mom!" Maia whined. "We haven't taken a vacation in forever! It'll be fun! Please?"

"We'll talk about it later," I said. "It's getting late and you have school tomorrow. Why don't you clear the dishes and then go read for your reading log." That would give me some time to talk to Jarod. He certainly had a lot of explaining to do.

In the meantime, I sent a text to Ted and let him know I'd be returning to work the following day, if that was okay with him. This break was nice, but it certainly didn't seem as if it was going to be able to last. The first step to removing Jarod from my life was going to have to be paying my own bills again. I'd been feeling restless at home anyway.

Before going to sleep that night, I went into my phone's settings and put the slide lock back on. I had unlocked it, and my computer not too long after the fire. I figured I was home, not really any need to keep the phone locked, right? Clearly, I was wrong. I wasn't sure of Jarod's level of involvement with the fire, but I was certain that he had been in my phone without me knowing. It was an odd feeling, knowing my privacy had been invaded that way. It made me wonder what else he had been up to. I'd spent so many weeks just sitting around, asleep or dazed by the painkillers. He had free reign to go through my things without me ever knowing. Well, there'd be no more of that. I grabbed my laptop and put a password on my profile as well.

CHAPTER 13

I woke up to the sound of my alarm, which I quickly silenced, to see Jarod peacefully sleeping beside me. Somehow, the talk that was supposed to happen last night never did. Jarod received a pressing business call regarding an out-of-state contract and ended up on the phone until after I'd finally gone to bed. We hadn't spoken another word to each other since dinner. I sat up and pulled back the covers, preparing for a shower and some coffee before work. As I got up, I heard Jarod stretch and yawn. He reached for me and then sat up upon realizing I wasn't there. "Hey you. You're up early. What's wrong?" he asked sleepily.

"Nothing. I have to get ready for work," I replied.

"Work?" He sat up, now fully alert. "Baby, you don't have to work anymore, we talked about this."

"I want to go to work," I said simply. I got up and walked into the bathroom, closing the door behind me. I didn't really feel like talking to him, not wanting another confrontation first thing in the morning and while Maia was in earshot. I wanted to tell him not to call me "Baby." I wished I knew if he set that fire. Even though I couldn't figure out a reason why he would do such a thing, something in the back of my mind said he had something to do with the blaze. I dropped my pajamas in the hamper and stepped into the shower. I turned the water up hotter than usual, as if I could scald off the growing uneasy feeling I had. I couldn't put my finger on it, I just had this nagging feeling I needed to get away from Jarod. Maybe I'd feel more ready to talk after work. It would be good to have something else to do other than sit at home and worry about what was going on with the fire investigation.

I jumped as I heard the bathroom door open.

"You can't even drive," Jarod said as he peeked his head into the bathroom.

"I'll take a cab or call a Lyft," I said simply. I didn't care what he said, I was going to work. I couldn't stay in the house another day.

"I can take you," he said. I expected him to throw out more reasons why I shouldn't go, so the offer caught me off guard. I really didn't want to ride with him. I was anxious to get a little space, but I couldn't think of an excuse fast enough.

"Um…okay. Sure," I said.

"I'll go put on some coffee," he said simply and then closed the door.

I sighed deeply and leaned my forehead on the cool shower tiles. The contrast to the scalding water was comforting. I felt so uncertain about my entire life. I'd been okay with my job (for the most part) until Jarod had made it possible for me to not struggle to make ends meet. I loved helping people, but I hated some of the heartbreaking conditions I'd find people living in. When I first started the job, I came home and cried fairly often. While I didn't cry as easily now, I still didn't look forward to seeing the ugly side of what people are capable of. The break from the job had been a welcomed surprise, and I didn't necessarily want to return to the gut-wrenching circumstances poverty in Baltimore's inner city had created. I mean, I didn't want to be a kept woman or anything like that, but I thought I'd have some time to reevaluate…maybe go back to school and choose a less stressful career. I sighed again, turned off the shower and stepped into the steamy bathroom. The cool air was welcomed on my heat-reddened skin.

I got dressed quickly. Well, as quickly as I was able to move these days. You don't truly appreciate the freedom of mobility until something happens and you lose your ability to move freely. Small movements you unthinkingly make suddenly become difficult, maybe even impossible. Initially, I hadn't really minded the loss of freedom. After all, I could have burned to death. But there was a growing sense of frustration and anger inside of me. The thought that Jarod may have done this on purpose…now I was feeling resentful of the pain, of the weeks on the couch, the weeks of physical therapy I'd been through, the months of physical therapy still to come, not being able to drive my car or run up and down the stairs. It's amazing how one thought can completely shift your perspective. How one thought can take you from grateful to resentful.

"Are you ready for work today, Mom?" Maia asked from the doorway. She had on her backpack and was holding a foil wrapped breakfast sandwich.

"I suppose I am. How did you know I was going to work?" She didn't seem at all surprised. She didn't look like she approved either, but I'm the mom, so she didn't have to.

"Jarod told me," she said. Then added, "Mom, you never told me he owns the company he works for. He says he told you that you never have to work again. Why are you going back now? We don't get it."

"Because I still have obligations and responsibilities," I said simply. How dare he use my daughter to make his argument for him. That blew right on the coals of my smoldering anger. I forced a quick smile and said, "Get going or you're going to be late."

"If someone told me I didn't have to work anymore, I'd take that offer in a heartbeat," Maia said looking at me like she was my mother.

"Well, I'm not you," I answered. "Now, come here and wish me luck," I said with a laugh.

She walked over to me and leaned over to give me a hug. "Good luck, Mom. If it's too hard to be there, remember you don't have to stay." At what point did she turn into me?

I gave her a quick peck on the cheek. "Thank you, Maia. Have a great day at school."

"Bye, Mom," she said with a quick smile and headed out the door.

I made my way downstairs to the kitchen and found a travel mug of coffee and a foil wrapped breakfast sandwich waiting for me. I almost said something to him about telling Maia about me going back to work and telling her about his owning the company, but I decided I just didn't feel like getting into a long conversation with him. I simply thanked him for breakfast, grabbed my bags, and headed for the car.

As he drove, I looked out the window thinking about how I didn't feel like the same me anymore. I wondered how my new function doing interviews within the offices of the courthouse would go. I'd been off of work for almost three months, so Ted had done some reorganizing within the office. God bless the poor people out there being interviewed by Paulette. She and I were basically switching positions.

"Desi, we need to talk," Jarod said, breaking my reverie and sounding incredibly serious.

"I don't want to talk about the fire now, Jarod. We'll talk when I get home from work," I said absently. I wasn't about to get into a time-consuming conversation and miss work. I'd been off for long enough and he had been avoiding the conversation for long enough. He wasn't going to dangle the carrot of answers to keep me home from work.

"That's not what I want to talk about," he said.

"Okay. What's up?" I asked in a disinterested voice. It's not that I wasn't interested…actually, that's exactly what it was. Once I know for a fact that you've lied to me, I don't trust anything you have to say.

"Do you know how I know you're the one for me? Why I love you so much?" he asked, still sounding incredibly serious. This was definitely not what I was expecting this conversation to be.

"Why?" I asked, slightly more interested.

"From the very beginning, you never asked me about my money. How much I made, how much I had…You didn't pry. I told you I was a welder and you were fine with that," he said.

"What's wrong with being a welder?" I asked.

"You'd be surprised at how many women lost interest quickly when they figured that I couldn't have but so much money as a welder. You took the time to get to know me. You're sweet and generous and loving. I can't imagine my life without you. I won't…" his voice trailed off. I waited but he didn't say anything else. How was I supposed to respond to that?

"Um…okay, well…thanks for letting me know," I said awkwardly. He didn't respond. He seemed lost in his own thoughts.

When we arrived, he absently gave me a peck on the cheek and said, "Have a good day. I'll be here at five to pick you up."

"Thanks," I said and got out of the car. I sighed and then made my way to the wing of the courthouse that housed my tiny cubicle. I was nervous for some reason. I guess it felt like showing up to the first day of school. Even though you know everyone, you still have a sense of anticipation.

Ted gave me a quick one-armed hug when I walked through the door. "Thank God you're back. We've been swamped." He made small talk for about five minutes, asking how I was feeling, how Maia was doing, and giving me the rundown on office gossip, how his wife and the crew were doing. Then we got to business.

The constant flurry of activity was a welcome distraction from all that was going on in my mind. When I finally looked at the clock, I was surprised to see that my lunch break had started five minutes ago. I hobbled my way to the cafeteria and got some chicken wings and salad with a water. I tried to eat healthy, but on the days they had chicken wings, I always had to get some. The cafeteria staff welcomed me back with a small round of applause. After I ate, I got back to work and remained busy until it was time to leave. Jarod picked me up from work at five as promised. When we got home, he started dinner, poured me a glass of wine, and insisted that I take a nice bath to relax after work. Maia was at her father's for the evening. Since the baby had been born, she wanted to visit him more frequently, and I was content to let her. It seemed that she and her father were working through their differences and she was in love with being a big sister. Every time she came home, she had a new story about some small gesture her little brother, Bruno, had made along with about a hundred new pictures. He was absolutely adorable and I was glad that she was getting to experience being a big sister.

I put my favorite bath salts in the tub, lit a few candles, turned on my mp3 player, and settled in for a nice soak with my glass of wine. I sighed and prepared for the epic relaxation I was about to experience. There was a light tapping on the door and Jarod came in to refill the glass. "I thought maybe we could talk about the fire now," he said. Seriously? Now? Epic relaxation was going to have to wait.

"Okay," I said, ready to get this over with. I watched him walk over to the closed toilet and have a seat. He leaned his forearms on his thighs and folded his hands.

"I did not set that fire," he began, looking me straight in the eye. "You know I'd never want to hurt you, I mean, I hope you know that," he added gently. Then he sighed and lowered his eyes.

"You're right, I did go through your phone and delete the messages from Detective Lembo. I set your phone to auto reject his calls and texts." He peeked up at me as if gauging my reaction. I kept my face blank.

"Why?" I asked simply.

"You almost died in a fire at my house. You've suffered so much pain and had to have surgery on your ankle. You might never wear heels again. You had a concussion. I feel guilty for all of that. I figured that the last thing you needed was that guy, Lembo, making you feel like all of this was any more my fault than it already was, you know, just because it happened at my house." He stopped talking for a minute, then added, "I'm sorry I lied to you."

"I don't understand why you would think I'd blame you for the fire if you didn't set it," I said. Shit happens from time to time. No sense in putting it on other people. I still didn't get the lying and going through my phone. If I didn't have any information for Detective Lembo, how much harassment could he have expected I'd go through? When I woke up, the house was on fire. That was about all the information I had to share.

"I'm not saying it was rational," he said. "You were in such bad shape, I thought that maybe if we added anything else to it, you'd leave me."

I remained silent as I thought about what I was hearing. Did I believe him? Something told me there was still more to the story than what he was telling me. Whatever his reasons may have been, he had violated my trust.

"I need some time to think," I told him.

"Can I get you anything? Is there anything you want me to do for you?" he asked as he stood.

"No thanks," I said simply.

"I really hope we can work through this," he said on his way out the door. When I didn't respond, he added, "Well, that's what I wanted to tell you. I hope you can forgive me."

Over the next few weeks, we settled into an uneasy routine. Jarod took me to work, picked me up, and continued to do as much as he could around the house. I could feel him watching me, like he was trying to anticipate my every need before I even realized I had it. It sounds nice, and most girls would say, "Sounds great, sign me up!" but it was...creepy. The more uncomfortable I felt, the more he seemed to try to fix it by doing more for me. He was bringing me little trinkets, cooking my favorite meals, and constantly suggesting vacations and outings, like he was trying to keep himself relevant and involved in my life. Like he wanted to prove he was indispensable to me.

After a few weeks of this, I began to get irritable. I had less and less to say to him. I found myself annoyed by him when I couldn't really identify a reason why. I didn't know how to confront him because he wasn't really doing anything wrong. How do you tell a guy that drives you to work, does the grocery shopping, cooks, and cleans that he's getting on your nerves? But the more he seemed to sense my irritation, the more he stayed up under me.

At work, I spent my lunch break thinking of reasons to break things off. Was I ready to end it? Was I ever going to find someone else that would accept me and my daughter? That would love me and take care of me? I needed some time to myself to think, but at home Jarod was ever-present and at work, I was busy from the time I walked in the door until I left. Just to get some time to myself after work, I asked him to pick dinner up that evening. I checked GrubHub to make sure he couldn't get it delivered before naming the specific craving I had. Before he left, he made sure I had my phone on me, just in case I needed him while he was out. When he left, I sighed a huge breath of relief. I paced around with the airboot off. I was supposed to walk a little without it every day. It felt so good to feel the textures of the carpet and the hardwood floors. My ankle was sore and stiff, but finally able to hold my weight for me to walk without limping too horribly.

I called Nika and Luna on three-way and told them about my troubled feelings.

"Do you still love him?" Luna asked. Her sweet voice was always calming and comforting.

"I don't know. All I feel right now is smothered," I sighed, rubbing my forehead.

"Girl, it's time to tell him to kick rocks! Not only did he go through your phone, he blocked numbers and erased messages. He probably read *all* of your messages! He needs to go!" Nika exclaimed. She was never one for giving too many chances. Jesse better make sure he watched his step.

"You're the only one who can make this decision," Luna said gently. "But know that if you're staying with him for any reason other than because you love him and you want to be with him, you're setting yourself up. You'll never be truly happy. But I can't tell you what you should do."

"Yes, you can! Well, if you can't, I can!" Nika said in a shrill voice. "You want me to come up there and help you pack his shit? I don't like how you've been sounding. You say you don't know what to do, Sweetie, I'm telling you. He has got to go!"

"When he asks me why, what am I supposed to say?" I didn't have a real reason. He apologized for any arguments we had. He never intentionally hurt me. He took care of everything. He even wanted to get me back into horseback riding. Shouldn't I love him? Didn't he deserve my love after all he'd done for me?

As if she could hear my thoughts, Luna said, "You don't owe him anything. If your gut is telling you to get away from him, you get away. If you love him, if your intuition says stay, then stay."

"Fuck that!" Nika interrupted. "Sorry Luna, but listen to her. If her gut was telling her to stay, she wouldn't have sent him 45 minutes away to go pick up dinner. He's lied to you, cursed you out, called you names and gone through your phone. And what if he did set that fire? What else do you need to happen to see what's going on? He could kill you! Stand up for yourself, Desi! Get out of there."

"You don't have to offer any type of explanation for your feelings, Desi," Luna said. "You're allowed to feel any way you want. You can't be in a relationship out of obligation. You remember all you went through before you finally left Maurice."

"Pshhh! I can't stand that asshole!" Nika interjected. "You shoulda let Nook Nook break his knee caps."

"What I'm saying is, a lot of heartache and pain can be spared by listening to your intuition. You already knew what you wanted to do before you called us. You don't need us to tell you what to do," Luna said gently.

"Fine, I'll play along with Luna's way," Nika said with a sigh. "What is your gut telling you to do?" she asked.

Just then, my line beeped. I glanced at the screen and saw my mother was calling.

"Hey, hold on a sec, it's my mom," I told them.

"Tell Mrs. Greene I said 'hi,'" Nika said.

"Will do. Hold on," I said as I clicked over.

"Hey Mom. How are you?" I answered.

"I'm concerned about you," she replied.

"Why?" I asked. I was doing much better than before. All of my physical therapy reports were positive. I was expected to make a full recovery.

"Jarod called your father and me today," she said. "He told me that he told you he owns that business we thought he just worked at. And that you've gone back to work even though he said you could resign and he'd take care of everything."

"He called you? Why would he do that?" I was floored. He called my parents to get them on his side, and apparently it had worked.

"He told me you two have been going through a rough time. He doesn't think you love him anymore. Oh Honey, he sounded devastated, didn't he, Earl?" I could hear my father grumble his agreement in the background. "He was crying and everything. I just felt so sorry for him," she said. "Sweetie, he loves you. You two have got to patch this thing up."

He actually called my parents and *cried*?

"There's a lot to it, Mom," I said. I always struggled with how much to tell my parents. They were convinced I was going to be murdered in some horrific manner when I moved to Baltimore. They pleaded with me to move to their scenic little town in Connecticut. "The schools are great and no one will try to carjack you," she told me. I wasn't willing to give up my career and friends just because I'd finally decided to leave my husband. So they worried. Every time I didn't answer the phone, it had to be because I was dead or dying. One time, I dropped my phone in the toilet at work and couldn't get a replacement until after I got off. When I arrived home, there was a police car waiting to check on me. I didn't want to rehash the arguments, the name-calling, or the privacy violation right now. I knew it would just worry them even more.

"Honey, no relationship is perfect. He says he said some pretty unkind things and he wishes he could take them all back. Maybe you should talk to him," she said gently.

"Okay, Mom. I will," I said. "I have Luna and Nika on the other line. They say 'hi' by the way. I'll call you back later, okay?"

"Sure, Sweetie. Just think about what I said. You've got a rich man who loves you. That type of stability doesn't come along every day. You wouldn't have to worry about how to pay for college for Maia. You could move out of that God-awful city. I know you have to go. Just…think about it, okay?"

"Okay Mom. Love you and Dad. Bye" I clicked back over and heard Nika and Luna engaged in a totally different conversation.

"I'm just saying, wait until Mercury isn't retrograde before you buy the car, Nika. You don't have to understand why. It's just better, I'm telling you," Luna was clearly on her astrology thing with Nika.

"So…he called my parents crying because he thinks I don't love him anymore," I interrupted. I was furious. This had gone far enough. Why was he trying to handle me? Why hadn't he come to me? Why use Maia and my parents instead of talking to me himself? And then to tell my parents about his money, like that was supposed to make everything he did and said okay!

"He did what?" Nika said in disbelief. "Punk ass…" she muttered under her breath.

"I hope that doesn't have any effect on your decision whatsoever," Luna said. "What he says to someone else has nothing to do with what is going on with the two of you."

"No. This is the second time he's used my family to try to get me to do things his way. I didn't see it before, but he's manipulative! Nika, you're right. He's got to go. Luna, you're right, I've known it all along, I was just afraid I was making the wrong choice, so I stayed," I said. I felt it in the back of my mind ever since the fight after the movie months ago. How many red flags did I have to see waving in front of me before I finally said "enough"? I was not going to stay until I lost my hair and lost weight again. This was over. Tonight. I'd give him a week to get his stuff out, and find a place. He could sleep in the guest room until he left. Once I'd made the decision, I felt like a weight had lifted from my shoulders. I felt more like myself again, like I was prepared to reclaim myself.

"Call us later and let us know how it goes," Nika said.

"Be very careful tomorrow. I don't think he's going to take the news well," Luna said. I guess she was having one of her feelings. I knew her hunches well enough now to know she wouldn't be able to go into further detail about why I needed to be careful.

"I will," I said to both of them.

When Jarod got home with dinner, I was already sitting at the kitchen table, waiting to have this talk. When he saw me, he laughed and said, "Damn, Baby! You're that hungry? I hope these crab cakes are worth it."

"We need to talk," I said.

"Well, I'm starving. Can we talk while we eat?" he asked.

"If that's what you want to do, sure," I said. I thanked him when he placed the plastic container in front of me. I waited silently while he set everything up, put hot sauce on his crab cakes, put butter and sour cream on his baked potato, and buttered his roll.

"Are you going to eat?" he asked, pointing at my untouched container as he put the first bite of crab cake in his mouth. "Mmmmmm! You were right. These are delicious!"

"My mother called me today," I said and the smile quickly vanished from his face. "She told me how you were crying and upset. You look fine now," I observed. And finally, I saw him. Everything was an act. He would use whomever or whatever to get his way. At that moment, I was fairly certain he had set that fire one purpose. Somehow, it had to do with keeping me. Maybe Luna was rubbing off on me.

"Uh, yeah. I'm sorry, baby, it was a moment of weakness on my part. I was all upset thinking about how much I would hate my life without you. You've been so distant lately. I just want my sweet, smiling Desi back, you know?" he smiled at me and took another bite.

"Jarod, I've tried, I really have, but I just can't trust you anymore," I said. "You betrayed my trust and violated the privacy of my home. You read my messages, deleted some of them, and blocked the investigator from even being able to call me, which meant you felt it was in your best interest to not have him speak to me. Those don't seem like the actions of an innocent man."

"Desi," he began, but I held up my hand to stop him. I continued calmly.

"You used my daughter to try to make me feel guilty about returning to work and you called my parents to try to get me to stay with you. I don't like how you operate. It doesn't work for me and it doesn't make me happy. I'm sorry, but this relationship is over. You can sleep in the guest room for the next week while you find a place to live."

"Baby," he began.

"Don't call me 'baby', Jarod. We're not together anymore." I was feeling calm and in control. I felt relieved to have finally done what needed to be done.

"Don't I have a say?" he asked me. "Don't you want to know how I feel about it?"

"You're certainly welcome to tell me, but it's not going to change what I've said. I don't like being lied to, yelled at, called names, falsely accused, or manipulated. This is how you operate, and that's fine. I'm not trying to change you. It's just not for me."

"Damn, so he's got you that good? Two weeks back around him and you're ready to leave me, just like that?" he was suddenly angry.

"What are you talking about?" I asked.

"I haven't figured out who it is yet, but you're fucking someone at your job, aren't you," he began to scowl harder. I watched him shift into that angry guy I'd seen after Byron Lee had paid me his visit a few weeks ago.

Calm down, girl. Don't get defensive, I told myself. This is all part of his act, and his act doesn't matter anymore.

"If that's truly what you think of me, then you should be relieved that I'm ending it now," I said calmly.

"I notice you didn't deny it," he pointed out accusingly.

"Right, because you always listen and believe me when you're in the mood to accuse me of cheating on you. That's worked out well for me in the past. I believe last time, I ended up on the floor." I tried to appear calm, but he was pissing me off. The crab cakes smelled amazing and I was hungry, but my hands were beginning to shake as they did when I was angry, so I kept them folded on the table where they'd been throughout the conversation.

"So you don't deny it. So why not admit it?" he persisted.

"Saying that you won't listen to my answer is not an admission of guilt. It's simply me recognizing a pattern that makes us incompatible. I will not spend the rest of my days arguing with you about my loyalty."

"You ungrateful bitch! I don't see him in here taking care of you and your daughter day in and day out! You use me to get financially stable and then just throw me out like garbage!" he screamed. Damn…and I had been doing so well controlling my temper, but the name calling and being hangry was too much for me.

"Your argument would be compelling if it made any sense at all! Since you seem to be incapable of understanding what I'm saying when I used big words, let me try again! I am not, correction, did not cheat on you. I am breaking up with you because *you* are a liar. I am breaking up with you because *you* seem to feel that conversations like this belong in a relationship. I am breaking up with you because *you* drag my parents and daughter into our personal affairs. I don't like what *you* do. It has absolutely nothing to do with anyone else! See how I'm not bringing anyone else into this? That's because the problem is YOU!" With that, I took the lid off of the container and took a bite of my crab cake. I'll be damned if I was gonna argue with him until my delicious dinner got cold. I didn't care if he saw my hands shake or not.

He didn't reply, so I ate in silence for a few moments. Then he said, "I don't understand. If it's not someone else, then why can't we work through this? Why does it have to be over?" He'd gone from angry to pitiful. It was like he was just searching for the right emotion to convey that would get me to forget I was breaking up with him. "You told me you loved me," he said.

"I thought I did. But now I realize I don't even know you. You change temperaments like most people change socks. I can't live not knowing what version of you I'll have to deal with in the next five minutes."

"I said I was sorry about your phone! I'm sorry about all of it! Please don't do this to us!" he whined. "We can fix this. We can work this out!"

"No, Jarod. We can't. That was the last time you're going to call me a name. The last time you're going to accuse me of cheating. I can't deal with this. I won't deal with it," I said much more gently.

"But..." he began, but his voice faded away before he finished the statement. He looked as if he was going to start crying. He sat, staring down at his hands, breathing hard as if he was about to hyperventilate. I sat there and waited for him to finish the statement. Eventually, it became clear there wasn't anything else left to say. Not now anyway.

"I'm going to finish eating upstairs," I said after a few minutes of silence. I quietly gathered my dinner and headed upstairs slowly to my bedroom. I locked the door behind me and then turned on the TV. I sat in the accent chair in the corner by the little round accent table and enjoyed my dinner with the company of Netflix.

The next morning I decided to drive myself to work. I'd had enough of the boot and enough of being chauffeured around. I was ready to reclaim my life. I hadn't heard anything else from Jarod since leaving him at the kitchen table, other than hearing my locked doorknob jiggle when he tried to turn it at some point last night. As I left my room to fix myself some breakfast before work, I paused to send Maia and her father a text to remind them she needed to come home after school to complete her diorama for a book report that was due the following day. I'd have to talk to her later this evening to let her know Jarod would be leaving. I knew she'd be disappointed, maybe even upset, but it was for the best in the long run. I finished my quick breakfast of toast with raspberry preserves and cream cheese, an apple and a cup of tea and then headed out the door for work.

As always, work was incredibly busy. I barely noticed how much time had passed until Paulette poked her head into the office I used for conducting interviews to ask me if I was going to lunch. Then, and only then, did I realize I'd left my purse at home. Phone and all. "I have to run home for a few minutes. Let Ted know I'll be back if I'm a little late, okay? I forgot my purse with my phone," I told Paulette on my way out.

"Sure, honey. No problem. You want me to just get you lunch today?" she offered.

"No, I need my phone so Maia can check in with me after school. And I have some errands to run. I really need my purse," I told her.

I made the fifteen-minute drive home, walked up the stairs of my porch with much more ease than I had in a long while. I already had my key in my hand, so I got in fairly quickly. I headed back toward the kitchen, then froze with a gasp.

Jarod was lying motionless on the floor in the living room. What in the world?

"Jarod!" I called. He didn't move and didn't answer. When I got closer, I could see that his mouth was open at an odd angle and he appeared to have vomited. His eyes were partially open and glazed looking. I couldn't tell if he was breathing or not. I ran into the kitchen and grabbed my phone out of my purse to call 911. After dialing, hurriedly giving my address and telling them what was wrong, and uttering a quick prayer, I kneeled by him to see if he had a pulse…It was faint. I still couldn't tell if he was breathing, so I leaned closer to his face to see if I could feel any breath. That's when I noticed he was holding an envelope with my name on it. I took it out of his hand, and opened it:

Dearest Desiree,

By the time you read this note, I'll be gone. It's clear to me I have ruined everything in the process of trying to keep us together. Clearly, you don't love me anymore. Before I met you, I'd been contemplating leaving this place. There's so much darkness and sorrow. There are so many horrible demons out there that want to destroy me. It's my fault, you see. I killed people in battle. And even though I should have been punished, I was rewarded with my business, which made me into something I never imagined I'd be. Rich. So because I refused to accept my punishment, my karma, God is punishing me now. He had me meet the perfect woman. Allowed her to love me for a moment, then took her love away. Baby, I tried so hard to keep you happy, you have to know that. I did set that fire. I wanted you to see that I'd always be there to rescue you.

To protect you. But it got bigger than I thought it would faster than I had expected. It blocked the original escape route I had planned. I'm sorry for everything I've done to harm you and others. I don't deserve to continue to plague this planet. Please know that I loved you the best way I knew how. My deepest regret is that I will never get to see your sweet face again. Never smell your intoxicating scent. I wish things could have been different.

Yours Always,

Jarod

My mind was reeling. He had tried to kill himself because I broke up with him. He had set the fire to try to keep us together! He was crazy! I stared at him, with an ocean of different emotions flooding through me. It was one thing to suspect he had set the fire. It was completely different knowing he had intentionally set a fire with me inside. I knew I'd be furious later, but for now, I just wanted the ambulance to hurry. I said a silent prayer and waited for what seemed like an eternity. The door was already open with a path cleared to Jarod when the EMTs arrived. They began furiously working over him as soon as they got there. After about forty-five minutes, they had him stable enough to transport. "It's a good thing you came home when you did," they told me. "He wouldn't have made it another fifteen minutes without medical attention. We need you to come with us. We have some questions to ask you."

This was certainly not how I'd pictured the break-up going. I didn't think he would take it well, but I certainly didn't think he'd try to kill himself. I asked myself if this was my fault. But I really didn't see how I had any other option. His behavior was too unstable. I didn't feel safe or happy around him. What I felt most of all, was relief. I was relieved he seemed like he was going to live.

I was relieved I'd forgotten my purse and had been the one to find him instead of Maia. But most of all, I was relieved I was no longer tied to him. I decided then and there, that I would answer all the questions for the doctors and police, then I would never think of him again.

CHAPTER 14

I sat in the waiting room of the hospital waiting for news. I called Detective Lembo on my drive over to tell him about what had happened and that I had a confession from Jarod about the fire. He was unavailable, but the desk sergeant promised me they would have him call me as soon as they could. The EMTs wanted me to ride with Jarod in the ambulance, but I didn't want to be stranded at the hospital. I thought about holding onto the letter until I had some time to think…waiting until Jarod woke up to confront him about it, but what good would that do? Was there really ever going to be a logical explanation for setting a house on fire to try to keep your girlfriend from breaking up with you? I don't think so. He nearly killed me. Then he tried to leave his dead body for me and my daughter to find. The more I thought about it, the angrier I got. He had almost taken me away from my baby, ended my life, over a dude complimenting me in the movie theater.

Finally, around 4:30 PM, I finished answering everyone's questions. Jarod was in stable condition. "We're cautiously optimistic," the doctor told me. "Your husband is very lucky you found him." I quickly corrected him and explained I didn't want any follow-up reports and that they were not to contact me about him. The stunned doctor simply nodded. I thanked him and left the hospital. As I was getting into my car, Detective Lembo called me back.

"I was surprised to see a message from you," he told me. "Did you think of some detail you hadn't told me?"

"Actually, I have a hand-written confession from Jarod about the fire. Apparently, he set it so he could save me and I wouldn't break up with him." I was so emotionally exhausted at this point that I didn't feel anything as I briefly described what had transpired in the last few hours.

"I'm sure you need the letter, but I need to get home to my daughter. Can I bring it to you sometime tomorrow?" I asked.

"Would it be alright with you if I come get it from you some time this evening? It might be kind of late, around 8:30. I'm tied up right now, but I really would like to get that letter from you so I can get this investigation closed out."

"Sure. I'll be home," I said. I was exhausted and numb. Above all, I was embarrassed. How could I be so terrible at picking men? How could I live with someone who was so clearly crazy and not have known it.

"You sure can pick 'em," I said to myself. I leaned my head back on the headrest and waited for the light to change. At that moment, I decided there was no possible way I was going to cook dinner tonight. I wasn't a big fan of fast food as it always seemed to upset my stomach. I decided if ever there was a time that I deserved some sushi, it was today. I went to a nearby restaurant and called Maia to get her order for the evening. "Yes!" she cried victoriously when I told her where I was. My daughter absolutely loved sushi. She had tried it at a party when she was four or five. She liked it so much she started requesting sushi any time I asked her what she wanted for dinner. "You never make sushi for dinner!" she'd cried one evening.

The restaurant was fairly crowded, so it took about thirty minutes for me to get my order. As I waited, I thought about calling Luna and Nika, but I didn't really feel like talking right now. I just wanted to go home, eat my sushi, take a shower and go to bed. Well, after I looked at Maia's project.

I sighed as I parked in front of the house. I left the boot off today. My ankle was definitely feeling tender. I ran when I'd noticed Jarod lying on the floor unconscious. Although I registered that my ankle hurt, the burst of adrenaline made it possible for me to handle the short run. I slowly climbed the stairs of my porch and entered the house. "Mom! Is that you?" Maia called from upstairs in her room.

"Who else would it be?" I asked with a chuckle. I talked to Maia and let her know Jarod had gotten sick and was in the hospital and he would be okay. I know it wasn't exactly the truth, but the truth was a lot to lay on an eleven-year-old girl. I hadn't given her any other details yet. I didn't want her to be alarmed when she got home and saw the floor in the living room. To my great surprise, when I looked at the spot in the living room where I'd found Jarod's limp body, I found she'd cleaned the floor up. I wasn't sure how I was going to break all of this to her. She had grown to be quite fond of Jarod and had gotten used to him being around the house. I felt even more miserable that I'd allowed her to grow close to someone and then have it not work out. What kind of example was I setting for her? Would she be angry at me? How would I explain the break up to her? Was I going to tell her the truth about the fire? I probably wouldn't do any of that tonight. Tonight, I just wanted us to enjoy the sushi and finish this project.

"I thought I heard you come in earlier," she said.

"You probably had that music up too loud in those headphones," I said.

"Yeah, I guess. Where's the sushi? I already set the table," she said as she clapped excitedly.

"Thank you, Sweetie, and thank you for cleaning up," I said. I gave her a quick peck on the forehead. "You didn't have to do that."

"No big deal. I clean up after the baby all the time," she said as she took the bag from me and said, "Come on, Mom. Let's eat."

She chattered about her day and showed some pictures that Cherrie had sent her of her little brother. "Look at him smiling in this one!" She smiled over the picture. I was pleased to see her getting along with her stepmother. I wasn't sure how things would go as she got used to her father's new life, but I had to admit, Maurice had done a wonderful job of making her feel included and wanted. I was grateful that the worst of our relationship seemed to be behind us. We finished up our sushi, cleaned up the table, and then headed for the stairs. Me, for the much longed for shower and Maia to continue working on her diorama. I peeked in on her masterpiece before heading to my room. One of the features that had sold me on this house, other than the yard, was the master bedroom. It had a small, but luxurious bathroom with a soaker tub and a separate glass shower. That had been pretty hard to come by in houses in my price range. It also had a walk-in closet. Everything was cozy without being cramped.

My phone chirped. "Be there in about an hour," a text from Detective Lembo read.

Perfect. That left me enough time to shower and change before I had to listen out for the door. I closed the door behind me and stripped, leaving my clothes in a heap on the floor. I'd get them later. All I could think about was how good that hot water was going to feel gently beating on my back. The muscles in my neck and shoulders were as tight as drums. I reached in and turned the shower on to give it a chance to warm up while I quickly used the bathroom. The shower was so wonderful that it gave me hope that the rest of the evening would go by quickly so I could get in my waiting bed and sleep diagonally across the middle. I smiled at the thought of not having to share my house anymore. Then, without warning, I began to cry.

All of the emotions of the day overwhelmed me. I was tired and sore and angry and sad. I was disappointed in myself for not figuring it out sooner or for getting back with him in the first place. I was such an idiot. I stayed in the shower until I was all cried out. When I stepped out of the shower, I put on my favorite periwinkle terrycloth robe, which hung on a hook on the back of the bathroom door. I stepped out of the bathroom and nearly jumped out of my skin.

Jarod was sitting on my bed.

*　　*　　*　　*　　*

"Don't scream. Don't say anything," he told me calmly. "I don't want to scare Maia or get her involved before she needs to be."

Before she needs to be? What was that supposed to mean? Something about the way he said it...I knew I needed to follow his instructions. Somehow, I knew this was a matter of survival. And that's when I noticed it. He was propped comfortably against the colorful pillows of my neatly made bed. His long legs crossed casually at the ankles. He was wearing sneakers without the laces in them. In his right hand, almost the way you'd casually hold a mobile phone, he held a gun.

"What are you doing here? You're supposed to be in the hospital," I said. My voice didn't sound like my own. It was hoarse and tight.

"I left," he said simply. I knew there had to be more to the story, but I wasn't going to pry. Nobody who just tried to commit suicide was going to be allowed to just waltz out of the hospital a few hours after admission. I mentally kicked myself for not giving the letter to just any police officer. I wanted to give it to Detective Lembo since he was the one investigating Jarod and the fire. Maybe they'd have handcuffed him to the bed or something if I had told them. "I was feeling much better after they pumped my stomach and gave me some fluids. Enough about me. We have to talk," he said to me seriously. "I don't think you're going to like what I say, but if you listen, you'll see it's truly the only way for things to work out for everyone involved."

He looked at me as if he was waiting for my response. I nodded, not able to find my voice. I was frozen. Not able to blink, barely even able to breathe. The clock on the dresser read 7:43 PM. Detective Lembo said he'd be here around 8:30. If I could get to my phone, I could signal him somehow.

"Look. I've given this a lot of thought," he told me in an extremely practical and calm voice "This is the only way it's going to be possible for us to stay together. Today was a day of revelations to me. When I thought you didn't want me anymore...didn't love me, I didn't want to be in this world anymore. The thought of finding a love as special as yours and then having to walk this Earth for the rest of this life without you...I couldn't do it." His voice took on a tone of dreamy wonderment, "But then, somehow, you saved me. When I woke up in the hospital, they told me what you had done for me. I realized it was just the fear talking. It wasn't you that ended things. I know Maurice hurt you, and you were afraid I was going to hurt you too, so you sabotaged us out of fear." Somehow, his entire persona had changed again. He was completely different from the sweet version or the angry version. This version of him was all practicality. All sensibility. "You proved something to me today, Desi. You do love me." He smiled. Clearly, he had read a lot into me calling 911. "I was ready to end it all. I had taken pills. There was no way I was going to survive, but somehow, you...my angel...you were there to save me. A love this strong can't be wasted. A love this strong can't be torn apart. I won't allow it."

I blinked but remained otherwise frozen. I stood there in my damp robe, leaning against the wall. I was cold, in part because I'd just stepped out of a steamy shower to a cooler room and I was still damp, but mostly, because I was terrified. I figured he was planning to kill me.

"So, here's the part you're not going to like…we're all going to have to die." He looked over at me as if he was hoping I'd agree. "Before you say anything or make any decisions, let me explain why. The soul is eternal, we don't really ever die. I want us all to be in this life together." I remained motionless, but suddenly felt even colder. He was clearly out of his mind. He was acting as if we were choosing between buying a Toyota or a Lexus. As if it was just a simple matter of perspective on whether or not he should kill us. I felt panic beginning to rise from the base of my spine. I wanted to scream for Maia to run, but somehow, even though he hadn't said it, I knew it would only set his plan into motion sooner. He'd kill me, then kill her, and then kill himself. No, I had to remain calm. I had to figure this out. There had to be some way for me to get Maia out. My phone was in my purse, which I'd dropped in the accent chair a few steps to my left. I had no way to get the phone with him right there watching me. I'd have to get him to leave the room. But how…

The moment sounded like it was supposed to feel so normal. As if there was nothing out of the ordinary going on. I could hear the washer and dryer going in the distance. I could hear Maia humming faintly through the door. She was down the hall… second door to the left. I could picture her with her back turned. Headphones on, head bopping to the music as she focused on constructing her diorama she'd been working so hard on. School wasn't necessarily her favorite thing, but she loved the chance to do the odd art project. In all her spare time, she wanted to do arts and crafts. Thinking of the terror she'd feel kept me silent. Kept me playing along as best I could. The longer I could keep him talking, the longer I had to figure out a way to keep Maia out of it…to get her out of the house. So I stood there silently and listened as he calmly sat on the bed, holding a gun, explaining why he was going to have to kill me and my daughter.

With my back pressed against the wall, trying to remember how I was supposed to breathe, I finally found my voice to say, "Of course there's another way. You don't have to kill us," my voice was hollow. Barley over a whisper. "What if we ran away together?"

"I love you and I'm never going to live without you again. By now, they've figured the whole thing with the fire out and now that you know, I'm either going to be separated from you if I go to jail, or if I let you go. You're a smart woman. I know I'd never be able to talk you into staying now that you know I set that fire. By the way, I hope you know I never intended for you to get hurt. I just wanted you to see that I'd risk my life to save yours. Only, the fire spread faster than I thought it would." He grew a little more animated as he defended himself for nearly killing me in the fire he had set. He really wanted me to be understanding of all of this.

Okay, think Desi! How can you use this to play along? He wants approval, you're going to have to find a way to seem like you agree with him. You're going to have to keep him talking, the longer he's explaining himself, the longer he's not shooting us.

"If I don't do this tonight, eventually, you'd figure out a way to get to someone...talk to someone. It's your job to get women and children out of situations. If I don't kill us all, we'll be separated." Damn. I'd been hoping he didn't think of that. Now what? I glanced over, my purse was unzipped, a terrible habit of mine. I could see my phone nestled in its compartment. How could I get my hands on it to call for help...

He stood up and began to approach me. He suddenly looked sheepish, nervous even.

"I...uh...I have something for you," he said ducking his head with a boyish half smile. He peered up at me through his lashes.

I somehow thawed my face enough to make my cheeks form a wan, nearly non-existent smile. "What?" I asked. Was this it? Was he about to shoot me? Please God, please help me get my baby out of here. He can kill me, but please rescue my baby!

Using his left hand, he reached into his pocket and pulled out a small, burgundy velvet ring box.

"Desiree Kane," he began to kneel, "Will you do me the honor of being my wife?" He smiled up at me. "You'd make me the happiest man on Earth."

CHAPTER 15

I just stared at him for a moment. Had he really just proposed to me? *What the hell?*

"Jarod..." I stammered. I had no idea how to proceed. Obviously, I was going to have to say "yes," but how soon after I did was he going to kill us?

I said another silent prayer. *Help me save us. Help me save my baby. Please, please help me!* Suddenly, Ann Rivera's words came to me. She'd told me that I'd know when the time had come. This certainly felt like the time "...you are brave enough, strong enough, and smart enough." And that's when it came to me. I knew exactly how I was going to buy us some time. As if upon hearing my prayer, God had delivered the idea instantly into my head. I was able to thaw from the frozen position I'd been in for the last fifteen minutes.

"Jarod," I began with a smile, "I'm so glad you recognized my fear. I'm so sorry I put you through such emotional turmoil. I do want to marry you, but look at me." I held my arms out and looked down at my fuzzy robe. "I can't marry you like this. What kind of bride would I be in a wet bathrobe?"

He smiled at me and stood from his kneeling position, then came closer. I forced my posture to remain as relaxed as I could make it. He took his hands and held me by the shoulders, I could feel the cold steel of the gun on my left shoulder. "Baby, you've never looked so beautiful," he said with a huge smile.

"Take this and put it on so I can see you in it just once." He held the ring out to me. I finally looked at it. "It was my mother's," he said proudly, then added, "I can't wait for you to meet her. She's going to love you."

"Let me dress. This is a special occasion for a girl," I stalled with a smile. "Let me put on some makeup and do my hair. I wouldn't be happy marrying you like this. What would your mother think of a woman willing to get married barefoot in a wet bathrobe?" I added. I was reaching. He'd never spoken about his mother, but I had to figure that no mother would be okay with her future daughter-in-law walking down the aisle in a wet bath robe.

"You're absolutely right!" he said. "Mama would want you looking your best! Go find your best dress. Do your hair. Put on some make up. But don't take too long, I can't wait to make you Mrs. Kelly."

"You can't rush true beauty," I said with a smile. "First, I have to find the perfect outfit."

"What about that black dress?" he asked. "I'm sure you look amazing in it."

"You want us to get married with me wearing black?" I looked at him as if he were crazy. Well, I gave him the look you give sane people when they say something crazy. "This is supposed to be a happy occasion."

"Well, you don't have a white dress," he said, deep in thought.

"I'll figure something out, just let me get in my closet." I looked quickly at my purse, but didn't want to risk him figuring out my phone was in there, so I headed into my walk-in closet. "I want to surprise you," I said putting on a sexy smile as I closed the door behind me. I breathed a sigh of relief to have a barrier between us, but it didn't really change my predicament. It just gave me a chance to break character and think. I already knew what I was going to wear. The pink gown I'd worn to Obama's inaugural ball. If I could find something to use as a weapon, I could hide it under there. It was a halter top with lots of ribbon lacing down the back. It even had a little train. I'm sure Jarod would love the choice. What I was trying to figure out now was if I should stall further by having Maia dress up, too. But if something went wrong, I didn't want her to be close to him when he started shooting. If he shot me first, maybe she'd run or hide. This would completely change the relatively stable life I had fought so hard to maintain for Maia.

If I could just get him to leave the room, I'd be able to get to my phone and easily hide it under the dress. I could text her to get out of the house. To find some help…come on 8:30! I silently prayed Detective Lembo was running ahead of schedule.

"I'm just so overjoyed that you understand where I'm coming from," he called to me through the door. "I thought you'd be upset with me."

"I know you're doing it for love," I replied. I had pulled the dress and shoes I planned to wear out in a matter of seconds. I was going through the boxes in the bottom of my closet that I'd never gotten around to unpacking, looking for something, anything I could use as a weapon. And then I found it. At the bottom corner of one box, I found exactly what I needed. I grabbed the thin, flat black box from the bottom of the cluttered box. Inside was a beautifully engraved letter opener that had been a wedding gift from my Aunt Ralona. It had Swarovski crystals worked into the gorgeous scrollwork on the heavy pewter handle. The smooth center of the handle read Mr. & Mrs. Kane. The point was sharp. I was sure I could do some damage with it. The letter opener had been such a beautiful gift that I couldn't bear to throw it away during the divorce, so it had been relegated to the bottom of the box and largely forgotten. Every once in a while, I'd go through the box, see it, think about throwing it away, but then I'd think about how much Aunt Ralona must have spent on it and I'd always put it back in the box.

I folded the dress with the letter opener in the middle and grabbed my shoes. I closed my eyes, took a deep breath, and stepped out of my closet.

"You're not dressed," He said, sounding disappointed. "What took so long?"

"I had to find the perfect outfit. Now I have to go do my hair and makeup. I don't want to get makeup on my dress. Most of it is in the bathroom," I said as I walked by with my arms full. I stopped by the dresser and got my undergarments, including a garter to put the letter opener in. "You know what I wish we had?" I mused with a smile. "We should have some champagne. This is such a special occasion." Then, hoping it looked like an afterthought, I grabbed my purse and said, "Almost forgot the lip gloss." As I walked through the bathroom door, I said, "No peeking! It's bad luck to see the bride early." I beamed my brightest smile before locking myself in the bathroom.

I immediately took out the phone, muted it and texted Maia. "Get out of the house as quickly and quietly as you can. Matter of life and death. Use your window if you can. Don't let Jarod see you. No time to explain. Get out, get to a neighbor and call 911. Follow my steps in exactly that order. Do not try to contact me. Do not come near my room. I love you."

Maia's room was directly above the porch. I hoped she could find a way to use the window as her exit. I had noticed a number of missed calls. Several from Luna and a few from Detective Lembo. I knew I couldn't talk to call 911, but I could certainly text Lembo. "Help. Jarod is here with a gun. He wants to kill us all. Hurry." Just as I hit send, Jarod began knocking on the door.

"What's going on in there?" he asked.

"I'm doing my hair," I said quickly. Then, I yanked my brush out, pulled my hair into a loose bun on top of my head, threw on some quick makeup, and began getting dressed. He seemed so normal in the beginning. Always so caring. He was the first of any of the men I'd gone out on a date with that I had allowed to meet my child. He was the only one I'd ever brought to the family. What the hell did this say about my judgement? What kind of mother was I if I let that be my child's story? Either killed or scarred by her mother's boyfriend? No. This couldn't be my baby's end, not for my sweet, creative, compassionate reason for working this job, buying this house, creating this life. I needed to keep him talking, to keep his attention to increase Maia's chances of getting out without being detected. I just hoped she noticed her phone.

"I think we should explore more options with how we can be together in this life," I called through the door.

"Now Desi, we've already talked about this," he said in a scolding voice. "If we don't do it tonight, we leave room for error. I mean, I get it. I know you're thinking I don't. Can't you tell how sad this is making me? I know it's not the way we'd planned to spend our lives together. It isn't the way I wanted it, but our marriage vows won't be dishonored…'til death do us part."

I silently cursed the psych ward at the hospital. How had they let him out? Was anyone looking for him? He was clearly not sane.

"My parents will be so devastated." Maybe appealing to my family ties would make him rethink things. I doubted it. He was pretty determined that we were all going to die tonight. I didn't care about myself anymore. I just wanted to get Maia out and safe. If I could figure out how to save myself I would, but if not, I'd be at peace knowing she was safe.

"I know this will be hard for your family and friends to understand, but when they finish out their lives, all will be revealed to them in the afterlife," he said.

I pulled the garter on and secured the letter opener against my thigh. It was cold, but the feeling was reassuring. I mean, I didn't feel safe; after all, I was literally bringing a knife to a gunfight, but it was better than nothing.

"But don't you see? This is the only way." He was pleading with me as he had been for the past thirty minutes.

"Why can't Maia go live with her father?" I asked. Maybe I could talk him into letting her go, although I prayed she was already finding her way out of the house.

"I've seen what a wonderful mother you are. I see how much you love your daughter. You would never be happy if I separated the two of you. And that infant of a stepmother could never take your place," he said practically. "No, Maia has to come with us."

"But what about your son?" I persisted through the door. I had to keep him talking. Keep him distracted. "You're going to be leaving him."

"The sad truth is that I had to leave him when I left his mother." He sounded sad. "His life won't change too much. He's all the way in Texas."

He was answering everything way too quickly. I had to find a way to stall longer.

"Come out here. I want to see you," He said.

"Just a minute," I answered in a singsong voice.

I checked my reflection in the mirror and made sure the letter opener wasn't visible. I jumped lightly a few times to make sure it was secure. I didn't want it falling out at the wrong moment. I applied my lip gloss and then, on a whim, hid the phone in the cabinet under the sink, and then opened the door.

"You are a vision," he said. "I'm the luckiest man in the world." He beamed at me like he really meant it. I guess as far as he was concerned, he really did mean it.

"Thank you," I said with a smile that I hoped wasn't too stiff.

"Wait...I didn't even think about this at the time, you didn't call anyone from in there, did you?" he asked as he walked past me into the bathroom to retrieve my purse. I nearly fainted with relief that I'd had the presence of mind to hide the phone. I'd put it inside a box of tampons. I hoped he wouldn't look in there. I doubted it. Guys aren't usually too likely to touch a box of tampons willingly.

I put on my best fake surprised look and said, "No, of course not."

He went through my purse seeming satisfied once he realized the phone wasn't in there.

"Where is your phone?" he asked me. The serious Jarod was back. In that instant, I understood that the whim to hide my phone had spared my life, momentarily anyway. I would have never been able to convince him I hadn't used the phone and he'd go through it and see I'd contacted both Maia and Detective Lembo.

"I think I might have left it out in the car," I lied smoothly. This was definitely divine guidance because the words were coming out before I even had time to think of them. "I was so exhausted and upset when I came in...I'm not sure what I did with it. Do you want me to go find it?" I asked innocently. If he let me, I could make it out to my car.

"No, I believe you." He looked at me hard for a few moments before the happy version returned again.

He held the ring out to me and said, "Now put it on so that I can see it on you one last time in this life."

"You're going to make me put on my own wedding ring?" I asked. At this point, I was fighting for every millisecond. If it stalled him, I was going to pull out every stop and delay I could think of.

He laughed and smacked his forehead. "Damn, baby, I'm so sorry. You're absolutely right. I'm so excited I'm not even thinking straight." He shook his head as if he simply couldn't believe his blunder and chuckled at himself.

"I forgive you," I beamed at him, "I just want everything to be perfect. Today is a special day."

"And my queen deserves nothing less." He took my hand and kissed it, then he slid the ring on. It was beautiful, I had to admit. White gold with a princess cut diamond that had to be at least a karat and a half, and two smaller, but dazzling princess cut sapphires on either side. The scrollwork on the ring was stunning. I would have loved to receive such a ring under other circumstances.

It would be the crazy man that's about to kill you that would give you the ring of your dreams.

"With this ring, I pledge my love and devotion. I promise to always honor, cherish, and adore you. I promise to take care of you in sickness and in health. I'll always provide for you. I'll always be here from you. This is my vow in this life, and the next. For all eternity. I love you." He looked at me adoringly and then stroked my cheek with his free hand.

Uh-oh, this is moving along too quickly. What else could I do to stall him?

"Um, I hadn't prepared any vows," I told him. "Your words were so beautiful and moving. Maybe I could have a little time to prepare some vows too."

"I don't need any of that from you. Your vows were in your actions," he told me with a smile. "You showed me today, with your actions, that you will always be here for me. That you have my back. That you love me. That's all I need to know."

I smiled back, but my mind was kicking into overdrive. In his mind, we were married. That was supposedly all he wanted for this life, which meant that killing us couldn't be too far off.

"I know you Desi," he continued with a smile. "I know you better than you know yourself. I know you're still worried about what's to come. I have plenty of training, baby. I promise you and Maia won't suffer. It will be over before you even know it began." He rubbed my back reassuringly.

"You know me so well," I gushed.

Come on, think Desi, think! What else is there? How else can you get another few minutes to figure this out? Or, how could you get him to put the gun down. Maybe get him in a position to stab him and escape?

And then I had it. I turned and began rubbing his chest. I looked up into his eyes through my lashes and said, "I can't wait to consummate this union." If I knew anything about him at all, this ought to buy me at least thirty minutes.

"Desi, you really have surprised me," he said with a pleased smile. "I really didn't expect you to take this so well."

"You thought I wouldn't want to enjoy my wedding night?" I asked playfully. I really don't know where all of the acting skills came from. In general, I'm a pretty up-front person. My face almost always gives me away, but somehow, knowing my life depended on it, I felt like I was going for an Academy Award.

"I guess I really hadn't thought about it," he said. I began to rub lower and lower, until I reached the button of his jeans. "This is taking longer than I had planned," he said absently, but I could tell he wasn't too concerned about timing anymore. Jarod always had been very easy to turn on, thank God.

"Well, we're not going to rush this," I whispered. I raised up on my tiptoes and planted a soft kiss on his bottom lip. "You don't want me to make this fast, do you?" I asked seductively as I put my hand down in his pants.

"No, I most certainly do not," he smiled. Without warning, he scooped me up and carried me to the bed. If he pulled my dress up, he'd see the garter with the letter opener. I don't think I'd be able to explain that away.

"Let's make sure tonight is a special night. I want to make sure my husband is well taken care of. Lie down," I told him, sitting up. He complied immediately. I pulled the floor length gown up around my knees. If I needed to run, or reach the letter opener, I needed to be able to do it quickly in this dress. I leaned over and began undressing him. "Why don't you put the gun down. I don't think you need it right now," I said. He hesitated, as if he was just now starting to think I might be up to something. I reached for his zipper and said, "You're not going to shoot me now, are you? Don't you want to feel this one last time?" I rubbed on his growing bulge as I asked the question, my face near is zipper.

"We're going to be so happy together, just you wait," he said as he sat the gun on the nightstand. At that moment, I saw a glimmer of hope that I might make it out of the house alive. One thing I knew about Jarod was that if he was really into it, he would prop his arms behind his head and close his eyes.

Alright Desi, let's make this convincing. I suppose the blessing of having been in a loveless marriage for years was that I'd learned to fake being aroused from time to time. I'd learned to be pretty convincing during those years. I needed every bit of those skills now, because I couldn't think of anything I wanted to do less. Well, other than being shot and killed.

Ordinarily, I didn't have too much difficulty with my gag reflex, but now, I had to fight the urge to throw up. I could feel the bile churning in my stomach as I took him in my mouth. *Come on, Desi. Get it together. This is the only way you're going to get him to close his eyes.* I wondered if I could stab him with the letter opener and then grab the gun. I'd never shot a gun in my life, even if I was able to move fast enough to get my hands on it, I would have no idea what to do with it. I know they have safety switches or something like that on them.

I mentally kicked myself for all the times Maurice had wanted to take me with him to the shooting range. I'm not a big fan of loud, sudden noises. I avoided fireworks and balloons. I found that taking my mind off of what I was doing helped me resist the urge to gag.

"Mmmmmm..." he groaned. I peeked up, but his eyes were still open. Not good enough yet...

If I stabbed him and ran, he might still be able to grab the gun to shoot me. I know the letter opener was sharp for a letter opener, but it was no knife. I was going to have to stab hard in a vulnerable area, maybe his stomach...If I went for his heart, I would probably hit his sternum. That would piss him off, but not immobilize him. Maybe if I stabbed him in the stomach and stomped or kneed his testicles...then there was always the neck...but with how I was positioned, I don't think I'd be able to do it quickly enough to have the element of surprise. I'd have to shift my weight and he'd probably open his eyes. The last thing I wanted to do was give him a chance to reach the gun...I think the stomach area is the best bet.

"Yeah..." he groaned. He was really beginning to get into it. His hips started gyrating. He stretched and put his arms behind his head. And then came the moment I was waiting for...He closed his eyes.

This was it! Now or never. Without another thought, I grabbed the letter opener, sat up, and plunged it into his stomach with both hands as hard as I could. He screamed and curled into a fetal position. I got up and ran with the train of the dress in my hand, ignoring my ankle. As I yanked the bedroom door open and saw the stairs just to my right, I had to keep going down the hall. I couldn't bring myself to leave without making sure Maia was out of the house. Even as I did it, I kept thinking: *If this were a movie, you'd be telling that dumb bitch to get her ass out of the house.* But I couldn't leave without checking, even if it meant my life. If anything happened to Maia, my life was over anyway.

I reached the door to her room and loudly whispered her name. "Maia! Sweetie, are you here?" No response. I quickly opened her closet and checked under her bed, just in case. Relief flooded me as I realized that she wasn't in the room. If I hadn't succeeded in doing anything else, Maia was out of the house and safe.

I ran to the window and looked down. Maia's room was in the front of the house, right over the porch steps. If I jumped, I was going to hit the concrete steps. I probably wouldn't be able to get up and run after that. I could barely run now...

"Desi!" Jarod screamed from down the hall. "Come back here!" I could hear him groaning in pain, but I could also hear the sounds of movement. He may have been trying to get up.

Shit. The only other way to get out was to get downstairs and go out the door. To get to the stairs, I'd have to go back toward my bedroom. I'd run without making any attempt to get the gun, knowing I wasn't sure I'd be able to use it and not being sure how quickly he'd be able to react, maybe even recoup.

"Desi! You fucking whore! I knew it! You were so convincing, I almost believed you! I knew you were cheating. He told you to do it, didn't he?" he raged.

No time for overthinking, the longer I waited, the better chance he had to regroup. I made a mad dash for the stairs, hoping

I could get out of his line of sight before he picked up the gun…
before he could take aim.

Just before I reached the top of the stairs, I saw him see me.
He was holding the letter opener in the hand that he had over
his bleeding wound, the gun was in the other. There was blood
dripping from his fingers onto my beige carpet as he stood beside
my bed. He lifted the gun and fired. Plaster exploded from the
wall near my head. The glittery, silver ballerina flats I wore had
no grip on their smooth soles. As I reached the top of the steps
and prepared to turn so I could run down to make my escape,
my foot slipped out from under me. I fell, landing on my butt
hard just as a bullet slammed into the wall right where my head
had been. Chunks of plaster and dust rained down on me. My
ears were ringing. It sounded like cannons had gone off in the
house. Without thinking, I slid on my butt down the stairs, as I
had playfully done hundreds of times with my brother when we
were children. My teeth chattered as I bumped my way down the
stairs to the bottom. As soon as my feet hit level ground, I was
ready to run again. There was another *bang!* as a slug dug into the
hardwood floor just inches from my left foot, spraying splinters of
wood into the air.

I knew without looking he was behind me, probably about to
make his way down the stairs. I jetted through the front hallway
toward the front door. My ankle felt like it was on fire, but I didn't
have time to worry about that now. As long as I could run, I was
going to run. But, where was I going to run once I got out? I
couldn't drive away. My car keys were in my purse, which was
still upstairs in the bedroom. I could bang on a neighbor's door,
but if they took too long to answer, Jarod would catch up to me.
And he might shoot them when they opened the door. I'd have
to find somewhere to hide. But where? The street was lined with

rowhouses, each with its own small square of grass in front. No cover there. I could duck behind one of the cars parked neatly in a line along the side of the street...

I yanked the front door open just as two more blasts fired behind me. The first one slammed into the solid wood front door. The second one grazed my left shoulder before punching a hole into the wood posts of my front porch, spraying splinters in my face as I ran by. The street was deserted. If people had been out and about, they'd probably taken cover. Although it didn't happen too frequently in this neighborhood anymore, things used to be a lot more active around this way. Before people had come in and flipped this section of houses, before I'd moved into my renovated townhouse, many of these houses had been abandoned. Decaying in varying states of disrepair. The residents that had been here before the revival were well trained in what to do when shots rang out. I doubted that anyone would be opening their doors now. It had only been a few seconds since his last shots were fired.

My heart was in my throat and I could barely hear anything but the sound of blood rushing through my ears. Still holding the long pink gown up, I ran across the front porch, down the stairs and across the street. I quickly ducked down behind the row of cars. As I pressed my back against a black Subaru, and I took a few seconds to gasp for air as I tried to plan out my next move. My shoulder burned, but the bleeding wasn't too bad. I would have to get that treated, but for now it could wait. I was directly across the sidewalk from a row of front doors. I was certain they'd all be locked, and if I tried to bang on one of them, he'd probably shoot me before I could get anyone to open up, let alone talking them into letting me in. No, I'd have to continue to hide.

I wondered what time it was. Where was Detective Lembo? He had to be nearby, right? Time seemed to have lost all meaning.

In that moment, I couldn't remember a moment before now, and I couldn't see anything after. I figured that even though it had felt like hours since I'd sent those text messages, it had probably only been about ten minutes. Maybe Lembo hadn't even looked at his phone yet. But even if he hadn't, by now someone had to have called the police with all the shots Jarod had fired. If I could just hold on until the police got there. They had to be on the way, one way or another.

"Desi!" I heard Jarod shouted from across the street. "I know you're out here somewhere. Come out, come out wherever you are!"

I fought the urge to peek my head up to see where he was. I attempted to rise to a crouching position, but found that my ankle wouldn't tolerate it. I crawled toward the bumper to see if I could get a quick peek of where he was. I'd have to stay low and be quick. A bubblegum pink ball gown wasn't the best camouflage. He was standing on the porch, gun in hand, calling out to me.

"Come on, baby, I'm not even mad. Well, that's not true. I'm mad, but we can still be together forever. I love you more than this. We'll sort this out in the afterlife. Besides, we'll all feel better when this is over! You stabbed me, I shot you. This will settle the whole argument altogether."

Suddenly there was a rustling behind me.

I jumped back but managed to stay silent. How the...I was staring into the face of Mr Byron Lee. "Baby girl, what in all the fucks in Fuckville have you gotten yourself into? This shit right here don't even make no kind of sense." He looked at me and said with a twinkle, "Not that you don't look ravishing, but if I'm reading this situation right, this crazy motherfucker done made you get dressed up and is trying to kill you and your daughter and then kill hisself."

"Yeah," I whispered.

"Shit. We got to talk when this is over. You need a lesson in love." He shook his head at me, an amused, crooked smile on his illustrated face.

I just stared blankly. Not able to comprehend what he was saying…what was happening. This whole thing had turned into some macabre dream world. For just a second, I was able to simply look at the situation for what it was. I was in an evening gown, bleeding from my shoulder, hiding from my psycho boyfriend who was trying to kill me, my child, and himself. He was screaming with a gun in his hand, staggering his way as he bled from his abdomen, down the stairs of my front porch. He'd left a bloody handprint on the same post with the bullet hole in it. He was screaming about how he'd be able to forgive me for stabbing him after he shot me. And now, I was sitting on the dirty sidewalk, dressed like it was the night of my life, talking to Byron Lee, the tatted-up drug dealer, about how I needed love lessons.

For just an instant, a silent giggle escaped me. How could this possibly be my real life? How was this not some crazy movie, or dream. I felt like I was in my own version of the Matrix, or a dream from Inception. Mr. Lee was the nightmare within the nightmare.

"Ms. Lady, don't crack up on me now," he whispered. He reached in his waistband and pulled out a gun.

"Desi! Come on out, baby! I'm sorry I called you names. I was angry."

Byron crouched around me and sneaked a quick glance. "He got to the bottom of the stairs. You know his crazy ass gonna come looking for you, right?" He whispered. That pulled me back into reality.

I could hear his sneakers scuffling across the sidewalk as he screamed my name, as if I'd give up and answer him. Like it was a bizarre game of hide and seek, and he thought I was going to give up and get shot.

"You shot him?" he asked sounding both amused and impressed at the same time.

"No. Stabbed," I whispered hollowly. I peeked. He was struggling down the step of the curb approaching the street.

"And he shot you? Most girls I know would have laid down and screamed and cried. You a soldier. I like that shit." He smiled at me appreciatively. Revealing a set of surprisingly straight, white teeth.

Having spent most of my teenage years on a horse farm hadn't made me street smart, but it had made me tough. I couldn't even count the number of times I'd been kicked, run over, fallen off, gotten slammed...you name it. It taught me I could deal with the pain later. It was going to hurt anyway, just get done what had to be done. Push through the pain.

"Desi, come on out now! Why do you want me to have to chase you? This shit hurts! This is how you do me on our wedding night? You set me up, got me all turned on, and just when the head was getting bomb, you stabbed me! How could you do that to me when I'm trying to give you eternity? Who's ever gonna love you like me? Huh? You'll never find another man who's going to love you the way I do. Because I'm the one God put here for you. No other man is going to forgive you if you stab him! Think about it."

Byron whispered a quiet chuckle and shook his head. "Baby girl, you done fucked up with this one. He's like...loony bin crazy." He snickered. "He screaming your name like in that Robert Downey Jr. movie, the one with Annette Bening. What's its name?"

"Focus!" I hissed to him. How could he be laughing at a time like this. Then suddenly, I thought of the movie, *In Dreams*. Robert Downey Jr. played a crazy man named Vivian, and had some sort of psychic connection to Annette Benning. Eventually, they crossed paths and he chased her through an apple juicing mill screaming "Claire!!" and sounding extra crazy while he did it.

"Desi! Desi!" Jarod continued to holler from the street. I had to hold back a snicker as I pictured Robert Downey Jr. screaming, "Claire! Claire!" I truly had to be losing my mind to be able to laugh at a time like this.

"I am focused, relax yourself," he still wore a crooked smile on his face.

Relax? Was he serious? How could I possibly relax in this situation?

"Desi!" Jarod continued to scream from the street.

Without warning. Byron stood up from behind the trunk of the Subaru. He fired a shot. I heard Jarod cry out in surprise and then fall. Byron walked out into the middle of the street and then fired a second shot. I sat frozen. "Double-tap motherfucker." I heard him say to Jarod.

Without saying a word, he reappeared in my line of sight. He was holding the gun by the tail of his shirt. I assumed he wiped it for fingerprints. Wordlessly, he dropped it into my lap. "You found it under this car," he told me. I stared blankly.

"Look Ms. Lady, I just saved your life. You know me and the law don't mix. You found that burner right there under that goddamn car. You got it?" I nodded mutely.

"Your daughter's with my boy's mama," he said as he pointed at Ms. Witherspoon's house, and then walked up the sidewalk and took a right at the corner.

I was staring after him, mouth agape, after he turned the corner. After a few moments, I heard sirens blaring in the distance.

Suddenly, I thought of all the Law and Order and Criminal Minds I'd watched during my time with my broken ankle. For me to sell that I had found the gun, I'd need powder or residue or something on my hands. I needed to actually fire the gun.

I held up the gun, pointed it at a tree, squinted my eyes and pulled the trigger. The gun exploded as chunks of wood spat out of the tree. I quickly dropped the gun as it burned my fingers. Within seconds, I couldn't even count the police cars. After another minute, there was a helicopter hovering over the scene, casting a bright beam of light. Baltimore City Police had just arrived.

Within minutes, detective Lembo had taken the gun from my lap and had me wrapped in a blanket. Where do they always seem to get these blankets from?

"Let me take you to your daughter," said Lembo after taking my statement down on his notepad. A crisp, white sheet, stained with two red carnation shaped blood stains, had been pulled over Jarod's body, which was still lying in the middle of the street.

My street was now unrecognizable. There were people busily working all over the neighborhood. The entire block had been quarantined with yellow tape that declared the area a crime scene. The neighbors had begun to watch from their porches and windows. It seemed like an entirely different place. The too-bright, white light of the police helicopter hovered above in the night sky. Little numbered tents were placed over the shell casings in the street. It all seemed surreal.

No one ever questioned my story. Although they were launching an investigation into who the unregistered gun with the serial number filed off of belonged to, no one questioned that I'd just lucked out and saved my own life. That shot in the tree? Oh, I'd done that when I was picking up the gun, before I figured out how to shoot it...before I'd fired those two incredibly lucky shots. Well, one lucky shot. The other, I'd shot him to make sure he didn't get up and try to come kill me and my daughter. I couldn't believe such a feeble story as me finding a loaded gun under a car across the street from my house was going unquestioned, but I was relieved and didn't want to spend too much time thinking about it.

I was released without being charged. After a tearful reunion, Maia and I were taken to the hospital. Upon getting my message, she had climbed out of her bedroom window, across the roof to the porch, and then lowered and dropped herself from the gutter. She'd sprained her ankle, but was fine otherwise. Somehow, we'd both made it out of the situation alive.

CHAPTER 16

She didn't want to leave the house for days after her release from the hospital. So she didn't. Days grew to a month. Maybe it was months…Time seemed to function different differently than it used to. Friends, family, and acquaintances had come to see her.

There were even reporters that followed her, shouting out questions as Luna had pushed her in the wheelchair to the car that would take her home. "Hero" they had all called her. They'd told her that she was "brave" and "incredibly resourceful" to have gotten her daughter and herself out relatively unharmed. What an amazing coincidence and stroke of luck she was able to find that gun. That she'd figured out how to use it so accurately. That's what they said, but she knew the truth. She knew what they thought of her. They were all thinking the same thing she was.

How could she have not seen how crazy that man was? How could she have allowed him to move into her home? Spend time with her child? Unsupervised time! What the hell was wrong with her?

She knew she didn't deserve the applause…the congratulations…the smiles…certainly not the admiration.

She was embarrassed…ashamed. Her relationship hadn't just fallen apart. It had done one of those sci-fi explosions, where everything sucked in first before exploding outward into a huge mushroom cloud of destruction and attention. Blowing a hole straight through her self-respect and dignity. Her story had made the national news headlines! They talked about her on ABC, NBC, CBS, and even CNN! The woman who saved herself and her daughter by giving a man oral sex before stabbing him to escape, then found a gun and shot him. The local radio stations were wild with comparisons to Lorena Bobbit, jokes and comments. Everyone who called in said they were suspicious about how she was able to just *find* a gun.

She'd never been a prude in the bedroom, but seeing it splashed across national headlines...on Facebook timelines. There were even memes about her circulating. It was all too much. Her phone was ringing off the hook with offers to be interviewed, but she declined all of them. She decided to spend some time alone. Her daughter would stay with her father for a while and she would hide from the world. She didn't even go out to the grocery store. She had everything she needed delivered. She didn't want to be recognized. Didn't want to talk about Jarod. Didn't want to think about Jarod.

She would lose time in her own thoughts. Staring off into space, so far tuned into her thoughts that when she'd shift her thoughts back to the present, she'd start in surprise at her surroundings. Sometimes she didn't even recognize her own room when she allowed her thoughts to return to the present. Well, allow was a gracious word. She had little control over where her thoughts would roam. She'd look at a clock and be shocked to find that periods as long as two hours had passed without her having done more than blink. She'd be that deep in her own head, yet she couldn't recall any specific thoughts she'd had.

Every single moment of this happened because of her lack of judgement. Her inability to choose when it was time to stay, and when it was time to walk away. Her inability to distinguish true love from the thing nightmarish movies are made of.

What kind of woman was she? What kind of mother was she? Who puts her child through something like this? If she ever even thought about dating another man again, she wouldn't even be mad at Maia for hating her. She was clearly no good at judging the character of the men she'd been around. She had refused to allow Maia to come back into the house for a few months after the mayhem, said it would be better if she got things fixed back up, but really she felt like she didn't deserve her daughter.

Obviously, her ex-husband had been right about her character...sure, not for the reasons he'd made up in court, she never did any of the things he cited as his reason for beginning the affair...telling everyone that she'd been having an affair, that she'd been abusing drugs. But he said that Maia wasn't going to be safe around her...Well, that part he hit the nail on the head, right? She almost got her killed! The man that she chose, allowed to move into her home...he planned to shoot their daughter. Who knew what type of way this would affect her growing up? She probably ruined her daughter's life. She was almost certain of it. She felt so much guilt, so much shame, that she couldn't even look at herself anymore. Whenever she did, she just stared, as if she didn't quite recognize herself. She stared cruelly, as if at an enemy. "You're so stupid. You're such a dumb bitch," she'd say to herself until her shirt was wet from the tears streaming down her face. She'd stare until she couldn't stand to watch herself anymore.

Even if she didn't openly say it, she always knew it...only her family could love her, but she probably managed to ruin that as well. What she did was...unforgivable.

She was so depressed she wanted to die. She didn't see any chance for love or happiness, true affectionate chemistry. There was no chance of her remarrying or having another child. She was stuck with this life. The one where her daughter would hate her. Where she would die alone. With lots of cats...well, maybe not the cats. Dogs. No one would love her for the rest of her days. She wanted to die, but she couldn't do that to her family, especially her daughter. How terribly selfish it would be of her to do that to her daughter. So for that reason, and that reason alone, she remained alive. But somehow, that made her even more depressed. Wanting to die, but not wanting to burden her family with the inconvenience of her death. Unable to move or eat some days.

She had been given a leave of absence from work, again, to heal, physically and emotionally, but she had no desire to return. She hated her job. Hated the things she saw. Hated what she had to ask people, and hated the answers they gave. She discovered being at home was no more comfort than being out, it was just more private. As she walked through the halls, she found she related everything back to that day. The hall was now the hall where Jarod had tried to shoot her. Her room, the room where she had seduced and then stabbed him. Every single thing about her life was now somehow related to that single relationship, that decision to go out with him. The decision to stay instead of stand her ground. The decision that had nearly gotten her daughter killed. And that one decision, the one that had led to so much hurt and pain, showed her she was not to be trusted. She would never again know male companionship. She wasn't even going to make new friends. With her decision-making deficiencies, it was a wonder she wasn't already dead!

When her leave was up, her shoulder long healed, it really had just been a scratch, she had to prepare to go back to work. She didn't know how she'd do it. She had become a shell, a whisper, a shadow of her former self. She was dull, colorless…bland. Without hope or happiness. And slowly, so slowly she hadn't noticed exactly when it had happened, but during her time at home, she slowly noticed that she felt a constant weight, sitting on her shoulders, pressing on her chest. She tried hot showers, long baths, and long naps, but nothing made it lighten. It was this ever present, heavy dark cloud. She wondered how other people couldn't seem to see it or feel it. It was as if the feelings of guilt, shame, and despair each had invisible weights attached to her spirit. It made her shoulders and back sore. Nothing she did now was without effort. Nothing alleviated the weight. It was there in her sleep, sometimes taking on form and swallowing her whole. She felt constantly drained. Tired of dealing with the world. Unable to relate. Unable to be who she used to be...unsure that she wanted to be at all.

That's when she discovered it. The different versions of herself, that she could wake up in the morning and put on like a suit. An entire body suit she stepped into...it covered her from head to toe. It zipped all the way over her head, like a mask with a bodysuit attached. There was Professional Desi, Mom Desi, Friend Desi, one for each of her roles in life. None of them were quite the same as the old Desi, somehow each was just a shade off, but if those around her didn't pay too close attention, she could pass. She avoided Luna like the plague. She'd have detected the fraud in less than a second. But with everyone else, she could put on a Desi and hide inside, peeking out through the eyeholes. She was hiding in plain sight. Working, mothering...hiding.

One day, she wasn't sure of the date, it really didn't matter anymore, there was a pounding on her door. Byron Lee was on the other side. He told her he'd been watching her in "a non-creepy way."

"Ms. Lady, you got to get yourself together. You ain't right," he told her seriously. He looked deep into her eyes, with his beautiful hazel eyes and softly told her, "My sister, you need help."

She wasn't sure which Desi suit to put on for him. He wasn't a friend and this wasn't work. She wanted to be angry, but this man had saved her life. She didn't have anyone to be for him but herself.

She prepared to tell him she had no idea what he was talking about, that she was fine, healed, good as new. She opened her mouth, but no sound came out. Instead, she sobbed. She cried so hard she couldn't even breathe at first. She began to let the emotions she had tried to bury and ignore flow freely. Well, *let* was a generous word. She lost control.

Byron pulled her into his arms and held her up as she sobbed. He was stronger than he looked because she was sure she weighed more than he did. He didn't say a word, he just stood there, held her, and allowed her to cry. After a while, he maneuvered so they were seated on the floor, and there he continued to hold her. She had no idea how long she sat there crying. It was as if the dam had broken and years of hurt, disappointment, pain, and anger were flowing from her. Some of the tears had been held back for decades. When she finished with the big, ugly, gasping cries, she moved into sorrowful weeping. He held her and stroked her hair wordlessly. With her eyes closed, she felt almost as if she were being comforted by her grandmother, long passed. Suddenly, the situation felt so familiar, she stopped crying. This didn't make any sense. Why was he here? Why had Byron Lee helped her in the first place?

"You ready to talk now, Ms. Lady?" he asked.

She stared silently, motionlessly for a long moment. Byron waited patiently, as if he truly didn't mind waiting for her to decide. Finally, she nodded wordlessly.

"I'm sure you have questions. You go first," he said.

"Why did you help me?" she blurted out, almost before he finished his statement.

"I wasn't about to watch you be slaughtered by some crazy ass motherfucker. What would I think of myself if I had let that man take that beautiful baby of yours away? I probably would have been able to sleep, but my dreams wouldn't be peaceful. I like my dreams peaceful." With a smile he added, "Besides, if my Mamma found out I knew you was in trouble and I let that man hurt you or your girl, there would be hell to pay."

Desi nodded, taking it all in.

"Why haven't I seen your daughter around?" he asked.

"I still haven't gotten the house fixed up. I can't have her come home to bullet holes and bloodstains," Desi fed him the same canned line she'd been feeding her family, her friends, her daughter...everyone for months.

He pulled out his phone

"Hey Rico," he paused and laughed. "Yeah, nigga we gotta talk about that later. What y'all doin'? Yeah, I need you to bring the truck out my mama's way. Need some repairs done." He paused again. "No. Nothing too major." He hung up. "They won't ask you no questions. They're real professional. Your place will be better than new in no time."

He looked at her and tilted his head. "But that ain't the real reason she ain't here."

"What if she hates me? This was all my fault. What if she never forgives me?"

"What she'll never forgive is you pushing her away. She needs you. You her mama and she's been through some shit. Yeah, you been through more, but she needs to see you're okay. She needs to know you still love her and want her."

She knew he was right.

"Ms. Kane," he began seriously, startling her. She wasn't even sure that he remembered her real name since he refused to use it. "You got to stop living scared. You can't be afraid to love. Scared love brings love you should be afraid of. That's the only way you can attract someone that screwy into your life."

He reached into his pocket and pulled out a business card. "This is Ms. Witherspoon's niece." The card read:

Angelica Sanders, PHD
Therapist, Friend.

"She won't tell nobody when you come see her. I think you need a friend."

He stood, patted her on the shoulder and began to walk away. "You still fine as all outdoors though. When you find you, I'm ready to pursue. I do love the thrill of the chase." His hazel eyes twinkled at her. He rubbed his hands together and then left without another word.

CHAPTER 17

I sat nervously in the comfortable armchair. Its muted browns, greens and blues blended pleasantly with the other muted tones of the modern decor in the office. I was in Angelica Sanders' East Baltimore office. The office was located in the end unit of a long line of row-houses on a busy street. There were apartments above the office, and a barber shop in the basement below it. The space was brightly lit with welcoming natural light. As I looked around, I noticed that there was no couch to lie down on, which somehow made me feel a little better. I'd never gone to counseling before, but I knew I had to do something.

I felt exposed. I hadn't felt like myself in months. I'd been avoiding my friends and family. Work was a blur. Byron was right. I needed to get myself together for Maia's sake, as well as my own. It still felt odd trusting him, but somehow I knew I needed to.

I finally answered Luna's calls and allowed her to come over. When she arrived, she didn't even seem to notice the bullet holes and stains. Or how pale I looked. Or how my voice was just a little different from the way it used to be.

"I know you've been avoiding me because you're not okay," she told me over a cup of tea. She was always so direct. She came over with some special blend she said would help repel the negative thoughts I'd been having. Luna always had some sort of tea with a purpose. It was never just plain tea.

When Luna gave me a card for a friend of hers that was a therapist and it was the same person Byron Lee had recommended, I decided to go ahead and schedule an appointment. "You knew that, somehow, I'd know. That somehow, I'd feel what you feel. I always know when something's wrong with you, Dez. You're hoping I don't feel it; that fear and anger still boiling in the pit of your stomach. You're hoping I can't feel it pressing in your throat. There's something you're going to have to say. Or something you need to hear. I don't know what it is. I don't have any answers for you. What I do know is you need…something. You need to talk to somebody. You need to talk." She nodded firmly as she said these last words. Then, with a triumphant smile, she added, "If you don't go, I'm going to call your mother. Better yet, I'm going to call your mother and Nika," she told me. "You've been moping around and hiding out depressed for months. I'm not saying get over it, but I am saying you have got to find a way to deal with this. You haven't even had your daughter come home. You're not okay. You know it, and I know it. And it's okay for you to not be okay. I also know the last thing you want is to have your parents worrying or Nika freaking out. I don't have any scary powers of persuasion, my friend, so I have to go straight to blackmail. Talk or I'm telling."

I called and scheduled an appointment that afternoon. The last thing I wanted was to hear my mother cry about not raising me well enough or telling me to go tell the whole story to my pastor, and I really didn't want to deal with Nika's wrath over me not taking care of myself. She was always on me to do more for myself. "You have to show yourself you love yourself," she always said when I'd deny myself whatever luxury service or item or trip she was trying to talk me into.

Byron's friends came a few days after he dropped by, and as promised, didn't say anything to me other than, "Good morning, Ma'am," before getting to work. They had the house looking better than it had looked before the entire ordeal. They repaired all the bullet holes, cleaned all the carpets, redid the hardwood floors, and repainted the wall. They even replaced the comforter set. The house looked better than ever, as if nothing had ever happened. They refused to accept any payment, telling me Mr. Lee had taken care of it. Maybe he was a little higher up on the drug dealer food chain than I'd given him credit for. Why was he doing so much for me?

It was time for Maia to come home, but I just wasn't quite ready yet. I had to find...me. I had to remember how to be me. Maybe *remember me* was a better way to put it. I felt out of sorts, as if I didn't know who I was anymore. Or maybe I'd never known in the first place. I always identified myself in relationship to others. Mother, friend, wife, social worker...but did that really define who I was, or *what* I was? Was there even a difference?

Maybe I really did need some help. I felt lost and lonely even though there were people around me. I just felt like I didn't know how to be myself anymore. Everything felt like so much more effort than it had before. I hoped this therapist could help me feel better. I just didn't feel like me. I didn't feel like making the effort of trying to be me. The Desi suit was heavy.

Just then, the door of the office opened and a tall, curvy, dark skinned woman entered the room. "It's so nice to finally meet you! Please, call me Angie," Dr. Sanders said with a warm smile as she extended her hand toward me.

She was much younger than I expected her to be. In fact, we were probably about the same age. Somehow, I expected her to be in her late fifties or early sixties. Her locks were wrapped into an elaborate up-do that made me wish I had locks. Her smooth, dark skin reminded me of the cherry wood tables at the library my father took me to as a child. Maybe it was all the books tightly wedged on the polished wooden bookcases on the far wall of her office that reminded me of the library.

I flashed a quick smile and squeezed her hand for just a moment. Was I supposed to tell her to call me by my first name too? I felt incredibly awkward, unsure of how to start telling this complete stranger my deepest, darkest secrets. How did people do this? I thought I was supposed to lie on a couch and talk about my childhood or something.

"I'm afraid I have you at a bit of a disadvantage," she told me with the warm smile still on her face. "I mean, of course, I saw the news and the paper and all, but I've heard the accounts of what happened first hand. I grew up with Byron Lee. Actually, I think you know my aunt, Ms. Witherspoon. Anyway, Byron told me about what happened. I mean, what really happened."

I just looked at her. Was this some kind of loyalty test and if I admit I know what she's talking about, Byron Lee kills me?

"Relax," she said with a laugh. "It's not a test or anything. I just wanted you to know that I know Byron shot Jarod Kelly in your defense, so you don't have to be careful about how you tell your story."

"Okay," I said uncertainly. I wasn't even exactly sure of what I wanted help with. How do you say, "I think I'm empty" or "I've been hiding in myself" to someone?

"I know this is kind of unconventional from how counseling usually works, and if it makes you uncomfortable to work with someone who knows some of your acquaintances, then I can refer you to another counselor." She had an empathetic expression on her face as she said this, as if she really felt for my position. "To be clear, Byron told me about the evening before your friend Luna even referred you to me. It's my intent to help you find peace with yourself. Everything we discuss is strictly confidential. In fact, Byron doesn't even know you're here or that we have any sessions scheduled. I just feel like working with me will give you a unique ability to be completely candid about your emotions regarding the events that happened."

"I'm fine with you." Why not go with the person who already knew the truth? It actually was a little comforting to have someone I could talk to with complete honesty.

"How well do you know Byron? Well, I call him B. We grew up together. I know you participated in the custody evaluation for his daughter. I doubt you know him much further than that."

"That's pretty much it," I said. I wasn't sure where this line of questioning was going. This certainly wasn't what I had in mind when I decided to see a counselor.

"Well, he doesn't tell people too often, but Byron is an empath." She looked at me as if I was supposed to know what she was talking about. Was that code for drug dealer?

"He intuitively picks up on feelings and emotions from other people," she explained after my blank stare.

"Like, a psychic? Like Luna?" I asked. Maybe that was what Luna was too. Even though she had always been that way, we didn't really ever talk much about it. I didn't understand all that psychic stuff, but I'd seen Luna in operation enough to know there had to be something to it. She said she'd been born that way and it sometimes made it hard to keep her head out of the clouds.

"Sort of. Your friend Luna somehow knows things, like events that are going to happen. Byron doesn't do that. But like Luna, Byron is able to pick up on things that you feel deep inside. They can't read our minds, but they can pick up on self-limiting beliefs, feelings, positive and negative emotions, things like that. Luna only told me she had a friend who was in need of help. Byron told me about the incident and about what he gathered from you before you ever called. This was just a coincidence, so to speak. So, we have a unique advantage here of me already having an idea of who you are and why you may have decided to come here."

Why was everything in my life weird? I couldn't even get a therapist the normal way. She already knew people I knew, and they just happened to be the psychic ones. However, I did find the idea of someone who already knew one of my biggest secrets appealing. I wouldn't have to worry about the carefully thought out explanation of finding the gun and figuring out how to shoot it just in time to save my life. My mind was reeling at the thought that Byron Lee was like Luna. But as I thought back to our conversations, it made more sense to me.

I felt overwhelmed at the thought of how many people could peek into my head, my heart and know the things I might not even know about myself. I wanted to know, but somehow also feared finding out for sure I was fundamentally flawed; that I was not quite enough.

"I'm glad you've decided to take some steps to help yourself," she told me with a smile. "I'm going to assign you three things to do for homework." I didn't like the sound of that. I thought I was going to get to lay on a couch and talk about things that were seemingly unrelated to my current state of mind, but upon realizing some obscure clue into my psyche, I'd be cured. This didn't sound like that at all.

"The first is to meditate for fifteen minutes every morning. You can use a guided meditation from the Internet or you can just sit and meditate on your own." That sounded easy enough.

"The second is to have something, even if it's something small, that you do just for you every day. The third is to keep a journal. Record your feelings, repeated patterns of thought, things you begin to realize about yourself and those around you. Do those things daily and I'll see you next week." This homework didn't sound too bad. In fact, I was kind of looking forward to it.

*   *   *   *   *

I began the next morning and followed the homework routine daily. The first time I tried to meditate on my own, but I discovered my thoughts were really loud and was pretty sure I was doing it wrong. But I kept trying. I sat there with my eyes closed trying to experience the mystical calm that people who know how to meditate seem to have. I just kept trying. I wrote in my journal and meditated every day. The hard part was figuring out what I was going to do just for me. I thought about a manicure or pedicure, but I didn't want to be out in public. I still wasn't ready to face people. It took ten minutes of standing at the door to talk myself into going out to see the therapist every week. Finally, I decided I'd try walking. Baltimore has beautiful trails that connect many of the city's parks. Trail-walking was something I'd wanted to do since moving to Baltimore, but never seemed to find the time. The first day, I drove to a point on the trail, parked in the lot and just started walking. It was surprisingly secluded. Eventually, I began to have the urge to run, so I started running on the trails every day. I wanted to be around nature, so I chose running on a trail in the woods. It turned out to be a good choice. The entire time I kept thinking about how I was loving the sounds of nature as I jogged on the worn path. I loved the sound my feet made on the hard-packed dirt, the crunching under my feet. The cool spring morning weather was perfect for a peaceful jog. I could feel the cool, crisp air entering my lungs, feeling the slight burn just before I caught my stride. I looked over to the left and was surprised to see small patches of white flowers peeking up through the crumbled, dry leaves.

* * * * *

"Have you been doing the journaling part of your homework?" Angie asked during one of my appointments. She smiled when I started using a daily dose of nature as my time for myself.

"Yes," I told her as I pulled my journal out of my purse.

"Have you been able to identify any thought patterns or things you didn't realize about your thoughts before?"

"I think I'm kind of irritable toward myself. And very sarcastic," I answered honestly. "Like, if something goes wrong or I drop something, I'm sarcastic and think 'of course you would do this' or something like that."

"What else?" She asked. She sat and waited patiently.

"Um…" I wasn't sure what else to tell her about. I'd begun to write about my refusal to look in the mirror. Well, not without feeling a lot of scorn and contempt.

"Do you know why I want you to monitor your thoughts?" Angie asked.

"I guess…so I can feel better about myself. Isn't that what therapy is about?"

"Not exactly. I wanted you to be aware of your thoughts because they determine the people and events you attract into your life. There are laws that govern the Universe, and in a manner of speaking, what you think about is what you bring about in your life."

"Is this like, that Secret thing? I don't believe in all that stuff," I told her.

"Your belief is not required for these laws to affect your life. Not believing in gravity wouldn't stop you from having to live with its effects." She raised an eyebrow and gave me a second to let that sink in. I remained silent.

"Relax. It's nothing scary. It's actually beautifully simple. You control your own reality in a manner of speaking. Your thoughts… your feelings are the thing you pull into existence. It's what you do with your consciousness and energy that determines all the outcomes you experience. Once you understand this truth, you will have the power to change your entire life. Every day of your life without you even knowing, the Universal Laws of Attraction impose their influence in every aspect of your existence. Everything from your career and finances to relationships."

"So everything that happened really is my fault," I said. Perfect.

"If all you do is sit around looking at all your mistakes and think longingly of how different your life could have been if you'd made a different choice, you haven't forgiven yourself. You haven't moved on. Your whole life's theme becomes your mistakes. Your 'poor choices' were the best you knew how to make at the time. Nobody consciously decides, 'I'm going to make the most fucked up decision I can possibly make,' but when you decide to live your life as someone who regrets decisions, you find yourself making more and more decisions that you regret."

"I didn't decide to regret my decisions. I just look back and… do," I said.

"We've been talking for months. I hear how you struggle with making life decisions. You worry incessantly that you're going to end up regretting your decisions. The Universe doesn't understand that what you worry about is what you *don't* want. What you think about, you bring about. You fear unknown complications and negative outcomes, then you manifest them. We've got to work on changing how you think."

We came up with a couple affirmations I would say to myself in the mirror several times a day.

"I forgive you."

"I make sound decisions in all areas of my life."

CHAPTER 18

One evening, she recognized she had always felt some version of the weight. For as long as she could remember, it was always there. She realized it was a combination of two very heavy emotions she had been carrying around: Judgement and guilt. From the second she recognized she wouldn't be able to give her child the stable, loving environment she enjoyed as a child, she felt guilty. Felt she had failed Maia. From that instant, her perspective was always feeling not as good. Not as good a parent as her parents. Not as good a decision maker as everyone else her age. She made decisions assuming they were in some way flawed. But when she looked at her present, without the bifocals of judgement and guilt, she saw she was holding her own. She was living paycheck to paycheck, but everything was paid. Her daughter was even in extracurricular activities. She was alive, happy. And so was her daughter. If issues were going to come of that terrorizing ordeal, they certainly hadn't shown their face yet. She and Maia got along as always. She must have made some right decisions to make it to right here, right now.

She realized how sometimes it's hard for her to look at her life, events, situations that may occur, through the lens of her current life. She looked at it through the past, comparing situations, emotions, feelings, phrases. It replayed in her mind with all of the obvious cues glaring, all the while thinking, "I hope it isn't that."

She felt like she would have to do something to alter the trajectory of their relationship, to make sure it never arrived to that same destination. But then, she realized she couldn't do that. This isn't then, it's now. She's not that Desi. "I'm me. Right now. Strong. Standing tall. I make sound decisions. Self-honoring decisions."

If she changed that, if she went back to what she was, made decisions the way she used to make decisions, she would get what she had before. The very thing that she never wanted to have again.

When she realized this, she fell into a deep, peaceful sleep. She dreamed of running in the woods, loving the sounds of nature as she jogged on the worn path. She heard her feet fall in a steady rhythm. The cool weather perfect for a peaceful jog. She could feel the cool, crisp air entering her lungs, which had a slight burn like the one she always got before she caught her stride. She looked over to the left and was surprised to see small patches of white flowers peeking up through the crumbled, dry leaves. She realized she was dreaming of her own life. What she had done just that day. She was living her own dream.

She woke up at peace the following morning. The weight had vanished. Her life felt unexplored and exciting.

She realized how learning to love herself and believe in herself is the best thing ever. She didn't have to worry about whether a man could love her, because she loved herself. And even if she didn't find a man to love her, her life was full of love. She had friends who loved her, she had a daughter who loved her, she had family, however far away, who all loved her. She began to understand it would happen when it was supposed to happen and released the desperation and fear of dying alone.

Angie had really hit on something with the journaling assignment. Desi was obsessed now. She began to look for the beauty in her life. She had an everyday journal where she wrote about her day-to-day thoughts. She began writing them in a gratitude journal. She wrote about the things she was grateful for, the good in each day, the things that made her smile and laugh. And the more she wrote about them, the more she found she had to be grateful for. She had escaped a deranged lunatic who meant to kill her and her daughter. How could she *not* be grateful? Her daughter had been spared the terror of being chased by a gun-wielding psycho. Her house was okay. She was okay. She beamed as she continued to find reasons to be grateful in her life.

CHAPTER 19

One Year Later

I smiled at myself in the mirror. My twist-out was looking fabulous. It was my first day as a business owner. I still couldn't believe how perfectly everything had fallen into place. I'd gone from a self-loathing hermit to a business owner in what felt like the blink of an eye.

A few months ago, on a whim, I decided to go visit my riding coach. She lived about an hour away from me on a farm with rolling green pastures and a beautiful brick barn. She trained horses and riders alike. Joy Harris had known me since I was about Maia's age. We sat in her kitchen and laughed and reminisced about people, horses, and horse shows past. She couldn't get over how tall and beautiful Maia was. Or the fact that she'd never been on a horse, which she immediately remedied by sending her out with a few of the other riders around her age to have her first lesson.

"I can't believe you gave up riding. You loved it so much," Joy said as she poured me a glass of wine.

"I just never seem to have the time or money," I told her. "When I got into social work, I didn't realize how emotionally draining it would be. And between court and home visits, it takes up a lot of my time."

"So, quit!" Joy said simply. She'd always been direct. Actually, blunt was probably a better word to describe her. "I can tell you don't like it. So why are you doing it?"

"I have to have a job. How else will I support myself and my daughter?"

"Do something else. Buy a business. Come train horses. Hell, go be a stripper if it will make you happy. You can't work for the next twenty years hating what you do and dreaming of everything you'll do when you're sixty-five. Live *now*!" Joy had been living her dream for over thirty years. She went to college to be an engineer, but after working for a year in a job she hated, she quit her job and started working as a barn manager. Her parents were shocked and appalled, but she was happy. Eventually, she was able to buy her own farm, and the rest was history.

"I've been thinking about what else I can do with my life. I definitely don't want this job for much longer."

We finished our chat when Maia came in with her eyes ablaze telling me about how much fun she just had. I hugged Joy goodbye and thanked her and went home. The next day, Joy called me.

"Do you remember Carol Parrish?"

"Yeah, I used to ride with her every Saturday." Carol owned a tack shop (horse equipment, for the non-equine inclined) not too far from where I lived.

"Well, she's been wanting to sell her business and her son is a vet in California and isn't at all interested. She wants to talk to you."

I called her that night and couldn't believe it, but what she was saying sounded doable. Now, here I was a few months later, on my way to my new business! I couldn't believe this was my life. I'd get to spend the day with the intoxicating scent of leather and talk horses to horse people. I had a set schedule and even had time to ride. Maia was also thrilled. She'd already struck up a deal with me to clean the shop a few times a week for an increase in her allowance. Things were definitely looking up.

The only thing I was having mental turmoil about now was Spencer Thomas. I'd been dreaming about him lately. At first, just a few times, but now I'd dreamt of him three nights in a row. It had been five years since we had our perfect night. I didn't even know if he'd remember me. I didn't even know if I knew how to get into contact with him.

"His number probably isn't even the same," I told myself. But after another dream, I decided to give it a try.

Well, it turned out his number was still the same. The idea of contacting him was on my mind for days, ever since I started dreaming about him. I had an overwhelming urge to see what was up with him, if for no other reason than to get some closure. Maybe he had caller ID, maybe he'd never deleted my contact information, but he answered the call without even saying, "Hello?" He jumped right in with, "This is crazy. I've been at war with myself about whether I should call you or not. I decided I'd give it one more week, then I'd call. Then I'd punk out. I wasn't sure you'd want to hear from me, so I kept putting it off."

That's how the familiar voice answered the phone. Holy shit. So all this time...he did still think about me! My heart did a flip-flop in my chest

"Are you okay?" he asked. "I saw the report on the news, but they never followed up to say how you were. You know how the news is."

For a second I froze. In my mind, I'd prepared for him to say "Hello" so I could say "Hi, I'm looking for Spencer Thomas," so I could check to see if his number was still the same.

I was aware of the old thoughts trying to creep in. I wanted to prepare myself for him to have no idea who I was, but I decided not to follow that though. But anyway, then he would say, "Yes" and then I'd say, "Hi. This is Desi Kane," and *then* we'd talk, but this was not at all what I expected. I had no idea what to say. I was drawing a total blank. I stood there silently with my mouth hanging open.

"Hello?" Spencer said on the other end. "Desi?"

"Hi Spencer," I said.

"I wasn't sure you were there," he said.

"You threw me off the way you answered the phone," I replied honestly. "I was expecting something more like the, 'Hello, Desi?' but you just started in the middle of the conversation and I had to regroup."

He broke out laughing and said, "Well, you're still funny. All these years, I still haven't met anyone quite like you."

"Likewise," I said with a smile. "So, how have you been?"

We talked for hours that night. And hours the next night. The following night, we went out to dinner and it was just as much fun and just as comfortable as it had been five years ago. Everything picked up like it had never ended.

EPILOGUE

She looked into his dark eyes as he slid the ring onto her finger. Even though she had sworn for years she'd never get married again, she cried like a baby when he proposed. The words "Yes, of course!" had flown out of her mouth without a trace of doubt or fear or hesitation. It was as if she'd been waiting for him to ask her all along. Somehow, she shifted worry and fear into optimism and hope. The relationship fell into an instantly comfortable partnership. They decided to save up for a vacation. They could both use one.

They took a four-day cruise, just a quick getaway to the Bahamas, and were walking on the beach. It had been a beautiful evening. They did some sightseeing and decided to go for a walk before returning to the ship. They strolled slowly, holding hands, talking about everything and nothing all at once.

He brought it up so casually, saying he knew she said she wouldn't do it again, but she had changed. Circumstances had changed. That was the old her. The broken version, the wounded and lost girl. She was whole and healed now. She was stronger, wiser, and most importantly, she knew who she was now. This new her shouldn't limit herself from what he knew her soul desired. He was always so calm and rational when they had discussions. She didn't have to worry about his reaction or censor her answers for fear they'd be used as ammunition in some future argument. She didn't fear where a disagreement would lead. She knew he'd never hit her or intentionally hurt her. She mused and said she'd think about it. She agreed she had changed and was confident in her decision making and confident in her decision to trust and love him.

She assumed they would continue the discussion later, but he gently pulled her hand to stop her. She looked curiously at him as he slowly lowered to one knee, his linen pants getting wet from the warm waves as they gently lapped the shore. Realization of what was happening hit her suddenly. Her eyes welled as he reached into his pocket, pulled out a ring and asked, "Will you marry me?" She began crying and laughing all at the same time as she answered, "Yes, of course!"

As they looked into each other's eyes, she knew with certainty he loved her. She knew with certainty she was good enough, more than good enough to stand here with him. She was exactly where she was supposed to be. She knew she enhanced his life just as he enhanced hers.

She looked back on how her life had changed in recent years. She went from depressed, bored, miserable and worried to the happiest she'd ever been. Changing her mindset had truly changed her life. She was joyously happy, self-employed and best of all, in love. In love with her fiancé and in love with her life. She didn't know what tomorrow would bring, but she was excited about the possibilities. She loved her life.

ABOUT THE AUTHOR

Aviyah A. Forrest is a lifelong resident of the beautiful state of Maryland. She lived in Prince George's County for more than 30 years. She currently lives in Baltimore with her two beautiful children. She has been a public school teacher for 17 years and is a National Board Certified Teacher. She was an avid horseback rider in her younger years and even competed on her college team. Summer is her favorite time as it brings a much-needed break from the school year and lots of time with friends eating Maryland blue crabs. Aviyah began writing after a very difficult period in her life. Although this is her first book, it is her sincere hope that it won't be her last!

CPSIA information can be obtained
at www.ICGtesting.com
Printed in the USA
BVHW070939101118

532602BV00017B/462/P